DEGENERATE

By D. Patrick Carroll

America Star Books

© 2014 by D. Patrick Carroll.
All rights reserved. No part of this book may be reproduced, stored in a retrieval system or transmitted in any form or by any means without the prior written permission of the publishers, except by a reviewer who may quote brief passages in a review to be printed in a newspaper, magazine or journal.

First printing

All characters in this book are fictitious, and any resemblance to real persons, living or dead, is coincidental.

America Star Books has allowed this work to remain exactly as the author intended, verbatim, without editorial input.

Softcover 9781611022094
PUBLISHED BY AMERICA STAR BOOKS, LLLP
www.americastarbooks.com

Printed in the United States of America

Other Novels written by D. Patrick Carroll and published by Publish America:

Diabolical

El Diablo y Los Santos

The Foundation Decision
(The Final Chapter of the Diabolical Trilogy)

Dedicated to:

Robin Ahrens, not because she's a degenerate, but because of her support and encouragement

PART I
THE DISCOVERY

I was taught in the second or third grade that Christopher Columbus discovered America and discovered several years later that <u>fact</u> was bull shit. Since then, I've questioned what I'm taught and what I've learned.

CHAPTER ONE

Doctor Madelyn Davies closed her front door, laid her hand bag and key chain on the entrance table and took off and threw her white lab coat on the divan and walked wearily to the kitchen. She filled a tea pot with water and placed it on the stove and then as she turned on the burner she heard a knock at her front door.

She thought it must be a neighbor since the building's security only allowed visitors to be buzzed in from outside. She gazed through the peep hole and recognizing the person, opened the door. Seeing the anguished look on her guest's face she said, "Oh dear, what's the matter? Please come in."

"Here, let me take your coat. I just put on a pot of water. Please, make yourself comfortable and I'll prepare the tea," she said, ushering her guest in. She closed the door, took her guest's coat and turned around to hang it. She paused, tilted her head and wondered how the person had gained entry into the building.

She felt something slip around her neck and then it began to tighten. She felt a tremendous pressure in her temples as she slipped into unconsciousness and her attacker guided her gently to the floor.

* * *

Mary Dinosa rolled over out of breath and glanced at the bedside clock. It read 7:15 a.m.

She giggled, "Whew, if I was a smoker, I'd light up now."

"You look pretty lit up to me already," her fiancé Ian O'Farrell chuckled, and laying an arm across her he pulled her closer and whispered, "Let me see if I can catch you on fire."

"Not a chance," she said, pulling away from him and throwing off the bed covers she added, "We both have to get to work."

She lived on the top third floor of a converted warehouse in a studio apartment located in the revived Hunter's Point District of San Francisco. The apartment's single bedroom was perched on a loft that overlooked a large room that was separated with a kitchen and bathroom on one end and a dining and living area that took up the rest of the space. Large floor to ceiling windows lined the far wall providing a view of the bay and a sliding glass window led to a lanai and a fire escape that descended to the alley below.

Her black and white cat, named Tux, short for Tuxedo and the brunt of many of her friend's limericks, slinked out from beneath the bed and followed her as she descended the spiral staircase. Midway down she abruptly stopped when she heard a blood curdling scream that seemed to come from the hallway outside her front door followed by a woman's desperate plea, "Help, someone please help me!"

She scurried down the remaining stairs and grabbed her Glock 9mm pistol from its holster that sat on a small round table at the bottom of the stairs. She ran to the front door and started fumbling with the chain lock and the two dead bolts. She could still hear the screams and moans coming from just outside her door.

She finally unlocked and opened the door and stepped out with her pistol raised to her right cheek. Squatted down in front of her and leaning against the far wall was a woman with her bloody hands covering her face.

Dinosa noticed her neighbor's door, just a few feet down the hall from her own, was wide open.

"What the hell is going on?" she demanded.

The woman dropped her hands revealing the face of a terrified young woman Dinosa recognized as the adult daughter of her next door neighbor, Madelyn Davies. Ian joined them, dressed only in a pair of sweat pants.

"It's my mother," the young woman said pointing with a trembling finger at the open door, "She's…she's been murdered."

"Ian, call 911 and stay with her please," Dinosa said with her pistol still raised.

She turned and looked through the open door. She stepped inside and other than a small over turned table and a purse and key chain lying on the floor, nothing else seemed to be out of place.

"It's the police! If anybody is here, show yourself with your hands over your head!" she bellowed.

She proceeded slowly through the room realizing how comical she must look, stalking through the room naked beneath her silk robe. She had been inside the apartment on several other occasions sharing a cup of tea or an adult beverage with her friendly neighbor. The apartment's layout was a mirror image of hers.

When she passed the staircase, she noticed a trail of bloody and blurred foot prints on the stairs and leading toward the bathroom. Seeing and hearing nothing she followed the bloody foot prints to the open bathroom door. Without entering she looked in and saw what appeared to be dried blood stains covering the floor and similar spots surrounding the sink's wash basin.

She retraced her steps, careful not to disturb the bloody foot prints and proceeded to and up the staircase, fearful of what she would find at the top.

As her eyes became level with the floor of the loft she stopped and that far too often feeling of dread permeated her entire body. All she could see were the discolored blood streaked legs of a woman from the knees down draped over the end of the bed. She took two more steps up and saw it was her neighbor, lying face up with her throat slit and her cold eyes staring at the ceiling. Her wrists were tied with rope to corresponding bed posts and her mouth was stuffed with what appeared to be a rolled up pair of socks.

She slowly backed down the stairs, not wanting to disturb the crime scene any further and returned to the hall where Ian was helping the daughter into Mary's apartment.

"I called 911 and reported the crime and the fact you were on scene. You're requested to call in," Ian said, leading the distraught daughter to the couch.

"I'm so sorry…I've forgotten your name…" District Attorney Chief Investigator Mary Dinosa started.

"It's Sara, Madelyn is…was my mother,"

"I'm so sorry for your loss, but do you think you can tell me what happened?"

* * *

Later that morning Dinosa walked into San Francisco District Attorney Valerie Kane's office and said, "Val, I want in on this Davies murder case and…"

"Settle down, Dinosa. I already cleared it with Chief Hamm and you'll be lead on the investigation," Kane said with a raised hand and waving the stop sign.

"Whoa, how did you do that?"

Dinosa and Kane had a long history together. It began several years ago when Kane was an Assistant D.A. and met Dinosa, a Homicide Inspector with the SFPD, while working the 'North Beach Serial Killer' case. They became friends during the investigation and the ensuing successful prosecution of the perpetrator. When Kane resigned her position to take an Assistant Deputy Attorney job with the Justice Department's thirteenth district she convinced Dinosa to join her as her DOJ Deputy Investigator.

As a team, they had successfully investigated and prosecuted several very high profile federal cases and had become somewhat of a legend in local law enforcement circles. Flying high after bringing to justice a home grown white supremacist terrorist organization, Valerie Kane decided to run for San Francisco District Attorney and won in a landslide. She once again convinced Dinosa to follow her and she became the Prosecutor's Office Chief Investigator.

"Hey, I'm not just a pretty little face in this job. I convinced him this will be a high profile case and we'd be in a better position to take the heat and that coupled with the fact the recent election shows I'm the most popular D.A. in the city's history, he reluctantly capitulated.

"He did say his Homicide Chief, Captain Halfhide, would be none too pleased, so Dinosa, as hard as this may be for you, you might be prepared to use a four letter word not in your vocabulary. Its' spelled t-a-c-t."

"I'll look it up in the dictionary. Val, you're amazing," Dinosa feigned humility.

"Okay then, where do we stand in the investigation?" Kane inquired.

Leaving her activities leading up to the scream untold, Dinosa related the events of that morning including her interview with the daughter.

"She was pretty distraught and I'll conduct a follow-up interview with her later, but she did say she had called her mother several times last night and the calls went to voice mail. She began to worry when she called this morning with the same result and decided to stop by on her way to school.

"She knows her mother's PIN to allow entry into our building and has a key to her apartment, so she let herself in and discovered her mother's body in the bedroom and panicked, retreated to the hall and started screaming. That's when I showed up."

Dinosa paused, looked at Kane for any questions and then continued, "Ian had already called it in and two uniforms showed up followed by Margaret Johnson and her CSI team and two homicide Inspectors, Frank Gardner and Marcus Jones. I've worked with them all and I can say Margaret Johnson is a well-respected, no nonsense CSI and we're fortunate to have her on our team. We used to call Gardner and Jones, Mutt and Jeff and when you meet them you'll know why, but they're adequate investigators.

"As you know, I've seen some really gruesome murder scenes, but this one has to rate up near the top. Poor Madelyn, she was a genteel woman in her mid-fifties. She was found on her bed bound with her wrists to the bed posts and gagged with a pair of socks. It appeared that she had been garroted and her throat was slit almost to decapitation. Her vaginal area had been mutilated by a sharp object, probably a straight razor or box cutter. CSI Johnson said she had been vaginally and anally penetrated. Bodily fluid she suspected to be sperm was detected and swabbed in both areas. We'll know more after the Coroner's autopsy report and lab results come in."

"Any signs of motive, like robbery?" Kane asked.

"Nothing appeared to be out of place or missing and there were no signs of forced entry. We'll have family members visit after CSI clears the scene to take inventory, but I believe this was planned and personal. There's a security camera located at each entrance to the building and we're in the process of collecting the disks now, but I know Doctor Davies well enough that she would not allow a stranger entry to the building or her apartment.

"Gardner is locating and informing family members and interviewing them and Jones is doing the same with co-workers and friends at the hospital. We'll know more after we've reviewed the security tapes and the autopsy report. Speaking of the autopsy report, I need to get to the Coroner's Office. They're scheduled to start the autopsy in about ten minutes."

"Mary, as soon as you can let me know the open cases you're working on so we can brief another Investigator and you can turn them over. I want you on this case full time," Kane said.

Grabbing her hand bag and heading toward the door, Dinosa said, "You got it. I'll call you later and thanks Val."

* * *

Marcus Jones stood astride the end of a long oval shaped table peering out of the window in an otherwise deserted tenth floor conference room at the University of San Francisco Medical Center. He had a bird's eye view of the Golden

Gate Park Panhandle and Kezar Stadium below. The stadium brought back memories of the stories related by his late grandfather, Charles 'Choo-choo' Jones. His grandfather had played fullback for the Forty-Niners when the team played on this field back in the fifties.

Marcus had wanted to grow up in his grandfather's footsteps but unfortunately he never grew to the physical stature of the old man. He stood about five feet six inches on his tip toes and was nearly as wide. He was glad his old high school football nickname, 'Squat Jones', had not followed him into later life.

His reminiscing was disturbed when from behind him he heard, "I'm so sorry for keeping you waiting, Inspector Jones."

Jones turned around and found himself facing a matronly looking woman with her hand outstretched.

"I'm Helen Lum, the Hospital Administrator," and after shaking his hand, continued, "Please have a seat. Doctor Harold Harris, our Medical Chief of Staff, should be along shortly.

"Hearing the news of our dear friend and colleague, Doctor Davies' death has us all a bit upset. She was a personal friend of mine, so I hope you'll understand…" she bit her lip and her shoulders started to convulse. She retrieved a hankie from her suit pocket and looking down, wiped away tears.

Composing herself, she looked up and continued, "I hope you'll understand if my comportment is less than professional. I promise to do my best."

"I totally understand, Ms. Lum," Jones replied consolingly.

An elderly man with white and red bushy sideburns and a bald shiny dome briskly entered the room. He reminded Jones of an older 'Yosemite Sam'.

After introductions were made, Harris stated gruffly, "Well, since you're a Homicide Investigator, we can assume our dear Madelyn didn't die of natural causes, so how was she murdered?"

"Oh Harry, must you always come off so gruff?" Helen said.

Jones removed a tablet and pen from his breast pocket and said, "I'm sorry Doctor Harris, but I can't comment on an ongoing investigation, but I do have questions of you two."

He continued, "First, what were Doctor Davies' duties here?"

"Well, besides treating walk-in patients at our clinic across the street, she was chief of our intern and residency program here in the hospital," Helen replied.

"Can either of you think of anyone who may have wanted to do her harm? Was she having any disputes with co-workers or patients that you are aware of?" Jones asked the obvious.

"No, no, everybody adored her. I can't think of a soul who would want harm to come to her," Helen said.

Jones looked at Doctor Harris who replied, "Nah, I only knew her on a professional level, but she was well and rightfully respected."

Marcus directed his next question at Helen, "Do you know if she had any romantic connections?"

"Not really," Helen paused and added, "I know Tom Jeffers, Chief of Maintenance here, would escort her to hospital social functions from time to time, but I don't believe they were romantically involved."

"I'd like to talk to him, if you could arrange it?" Jones asked Helen.

"Of course," she replied.

"I'll also need a list of all the other people she worked with or had personal or professional contact with, if you could be so kind?"

"Of course," Helen nodded.

"I'll also need both of your work phone numbers, your home numbers and, if you have one, your cell numbers," Jones stated.

"Why would you have the need to disturb me at home?" Doctor Harris asked defensively.

"We probably won't have a need to bother you at all, Doctor Harris. It's a routine request, but if I have to I can get a court order and get the numbers from the hospital's personnel records…" Jones said evenly. This arrogant asshole is starting to piss me off, he thought.

"Very well," Doctor Harris grumbled as he scribbled on a pad of paper, ripped off the sheet and handed it to Jones and concluded, "If that's it, I have work to do."

"That'll do for now. We'll be in touch," Jones said, maintaining his cool.

After the good doctor left, Helen said demurely, "I must apologize for Doctor Harris' behavior. He's been a pain in my…ah…posterior for years."

"Not a problem, ma'am. I know you're a very busy woman, but we'll need to keep an open line of communication and it won't always require I talk directly to you. Do you have anyone on your staff that could act as a go-between?" Jones asked.

"That's very considerate of you Inspector, and as a matter of fact I do. If you'll walk down the hall with me, I'll introduce you to my Administrative Assistant."

Together they walked out of the conference room and down the hall to a door marked 'Administrator', with 'Helen Lum, PHD' written underneath and walked into an outer office. A very attractive African American woman with a short afro hair cut in her mid to late twenties sat behind the desk.

"Elena, this is SFPD Inspector Marcus Jones. He's investigating the murder of our dear Doctor Davies. Inspector Jones, this is my assistant, Elena Wyeth."

Elena stood and extended her hand across the desk, and Marcus thought, holy shit, she's beautiful. This could be my lucky day when she said, "Pleasure to meet you."

"Y-yes, of course," Marcus stuttered and was flustered because he didn't have a clever come back.

"If Inspector Marcus should call, I'd like you to extend him all courtesies and act as my communicator. You'll be my liaison with his department," Helen said.

"Yes, Ma'am," Elena replied.

* * *

Dinosa stepped out of the elevator at the basement level of the SFPD Headquarters Building, 850 Bryant Street. The basement was reserved for records and evidence storage and also contained the County Morgue and Coroner's Office. She walked down the hall until she came to a door marked 'Coroner's Office, Rolf Zeller, MD, Chief Medical Examiner' and entered.

She was greeted by a middle aged woman from behind a desk whose name tag identified her as Jamaica Roundtree, and her name described her perfectly. She was a large black woman and her beaming face told anyone why she was called 'Auntie' by many.

"Why Inspector Mary, it's so nice to see you. It's been a long time," she cried.

She stood up and waddled around her desk and gave Dinosa a big bear hug.

"It's good to see you too, Jamaica," Dinosa replied and returned the hug.

"Doctor Zeller said you would be here. He and the others are waiting for you in the scrub room."

Dinosa proceeded through another door where she was greeted by a familiar and friendly face in the scrub and gown up room, CSI Margaret Johnson.

"God Mary, how many times have we met in this room?" she asked rhetorically.

"Too many," Dinosa replied and continued, "We didn't get a chance to chat earlier, but I thought you were turning your papers in several years ago, after the Barnes family case."

She was referring to the massacre of an entire family in the Avenues that left everyone involved in the investigation, including the seasoned Margaret Johnson, with images that still haunted them.

"I did, but after six months of sitting in an empty nest and staring at the old man, I decided the Department's need for my expertise was more important than my exciting retirement. In other words, I was bored to death," Margaret sighed.

"Well, the old man's loss is our gain," Dinosa smiled, pointed over her shoulder and under her breath added, "Who's the he-man?"

Bent over and struggling to keep his balance while trying to put on surgical shoe covers was a giant of a man. Dinosa was intrigued. The six foot six or seven inch man had no neck and shoulders so wide he'd have to turn sideways to traverse a narrow hallway. His torso tapered down to a waist size many women would be envious of.

"Oh," Johnson said turning toward the giant, "I take it you two haven't met. DA Investigator Mary Dinosa, meet Homicide Inspector Arnold Lassiter."

The two took a step toward each other and the arm of the two sizes too small surgical gown ripped as Arnold extended his hand. Dinosa thought he did resemble the original Arnold, but hoped he was a better actor. She snickered to herself at the thought.

"Damn, they just don't make these in my size," he said awkwardly and finished, "It's nice to meet you. Captain Halfhide assigned me to work with you on the Davies case."

"Don't you mean he assigned you to keep an eye on me and be his conduit?" Dinosa sneered.

"Exactly," Lassiter smiled and continued, "But I also hope I can be of some help."

At least the ape is honest, Dinosa thought.

After they were all gowned and wearing surgical caps and masks, they entered the autopsy suite where Doctor Zeller and a tall gorgeous young woman stood behind the nearest table where the naked and discolored body of Madelyn Davies laid. Dinosa assumed the tall striking red head was Doctor Zeller's assistant.

"It's about god damned time you got here Dinosa! I'd like to eat dinner sometime tonight," Doctor Zeller bellowed from behind a surgical mask.

Dinosa looked at the clock on the wall which read 3:05 pm and replied, "Fuck you Doc, and be happy I'm only five minutes late. By the way, it's good to see you too."

"Well, let's get restarted. Unless the toxicology tests prove different, I've already determined the cause of death," he paused to make a scalpel incision starting at Madelyn's thorax and continued down to her pelvis.

"Are you going to keep us in suspense?" Dinosa groaned.

"Cause of death was exsanguination, she f'n bled to death. This slice across her throat severed her carotid and juggler. She would have been dead in less than a minute," he answered.

"What about the garroted marks. They penetrated the skin," Dinosa remarked.

"Dinosa, stick with your inspectoring and leave the science to us who are trained, will ya? It appears this bastard used some kind of a cord to strangle her into unconsciousness. It did not penetrate the skin, but it did leave contusion paths and based on number of paths, it's my professional opinion, this degenerate son of a bitch tortured this poor woman by allowing her to revive while he was raping her, strangling her into unconsciousness again, and allowing her to revive. He made her watch him and feel the pain as he mutilated her privates. These wounds occurred pre-mortem.

"The near decapitation was the coup d' grass and mercifully ended her misery. This is one sick fucker," he concluded.

"We didn't find a murder weapon, any ideas?" Dinosa asked.

"The only thing I know that could make these incisions is a surgical scalpel and it was yielded by someone who knew what he was doing. He incised and removed the labia and unless you've got it, its' missing. He probably took it as some kind of trophy," Doctor Zeller replied.

"Dean, you should stick to your autopsying and leave the speculation to us who are trained," Dinosa retorted with an exaggerated sigh.

"Margaret gave us a time of death based on liver temp as between 8:00 pm and 10:00pm last night. Can you narrow that window?" Dinosa inquired.

"Well, I'm about to open her stomach. If you can tell me when she ate her last meal I might be able to get the time of death give or take half an hour based on the digestive breakdown," he said.

"Okay, I'm out of here," Dinosa said.

Lassiter and Johnson followed her out of autopsy and as they disrobed the gowns and footwear he asked, "Aren't you supposed to stay until the end?"

"How many autopsies have you attended?" Dinosa asked incredulously.

"Zero," Lassiter said and quickly added, "I just transferred in from White Collar."

"Oh, isn't that sweet? Well, if you want to smell the most gut wrenching odor of your life, be my guest and go back in there while he opens up her stomach and colon."

* * *

CHAPTER TWO

At 9:00 am the following morning the three Homicide Inspectors and D.A. Inspector Mary Dinosa were crowded into a small conference room on the fourth floor 'Homicide Division' at 850 Bryant Street. They were gathered around a monitor looking at a view of the entrance in the garage to Dinosa's and Davies' apartment building.

"That's Doctor Davies," Dinosa said as they watched the Doctor approach the entrance door in the parking garage and punch in her PIN, open the door and enter the building. It opened outward and as it slowly began to close a figure dressed in a dark gray trench coat and wearing a knitted ski mask and dark colored gloves came into view and caught the door just before it latched.

The figure looked down and away from the camera and stood motionless for a good minute before cracking the door, peeking in and then disappearing inside. The video time stamp read 8:53 pm.

"Rewind that and everybody keep a keen eye on our killer and see if you can detect any identifying clues, his height, his build, his shoes, his stride or any detectable mannerisms," Dinosa said.

They reran the scene two more times and Jones said, "It shouldn't be difficult to determine his exact height when we measure the door and compare it to him, but if it's a standard seven foot door, I'd guess he's between five feet ten inches and six foot."

"The white and orange tennis shoes look like a pair of Nike's I own and they are very popular and can be purchased a fair number of different stores in the city alone. We can get a positive brand identification and approximate size after our IT people process this clip," Inspector Gardner contributed.

Dinosa craned her neck to one side and said, "He didn't look nervous or in any way concerned that someone may come upon him. This is a real cool prick, considering what he's about to do. He must have been stalking her. He knew when she would be arriving or followed her home and knew her habits. This guy acts like a pro, but if its' a professional hit, why would he rape and mutilate her?"

"I never heard of a professional hit man that would leave his semen at the crime scene," Arnold said sheepishly.

Dinosa thought, what a fucking genius this guy is, but didn't say it and that surprised her. Was she getting soft, she wondered.

"Is that the only video camera in the building?" Jones asked.

"No, there's another one at the front door entrance, but there are none inside the building. They feed the surveillance video to each apartment so the resident can see their visitor and buzz them in," Dinosa said and a thought prompted her to add, "Lassiter, I want you to watch the disks from both cameras and go back at least forty-eight hours prior to the murder and see if you can pick up anything suspicious."

They fast forwarded the videos and did not observe anyone entering or leaving from the garage entrance except for Dinosa and her fiancé entering from the front door entrance at 10:06 pm and the first responders, two uniform patrolmen at 7:28 the following morning.

"The son of a bitch must have left through the patio door and down the fire escape," Dinosa noted.

Looking at Gardner and Jones she asked, "Okay, did you guys dig up anything in your interviews?"

"I talked to the hospital administrator, Helen Lum and the chief of staff there, Doctor Harold Harris. Doctor Harris was a dick, but Ms. Lum was congenial and cooperative.

"Doctor Davies was on the hospital staff and treated patients at their clinic and oversaw their intern and residency program. Ms. Lum and her assistant have arranged for me to interview each of the interns and residents today and I'll be meeting with the clinic staff tomorrow," Jones replied and added, "I reviewed the parking lot cameras and they show her leaving the hospital at 8:25 pm.

Dinosa looked at Gardner who said, "Doctor Davies didn't have a lot of living family. Her parents as well as an older brother are deceased. Aside from some distant cousins, her daughter Sara is her only living relative. She's ten years divorced from Sara's father who lives in upstate New York. I'm still confirming his alibi."

"Well, we have the victim's time line from when she left the hospital. Considering the time it would take her to get home from the hospital, I believe we can say she didn't make any stops. Determine the time line leading up to her leaving the hospital. Lassiter here is our designated video expert, so take him along with you today and see if you can follow her movements and who she met with the day of the murder. Hospital cameras should assist you," Dinosa said.

Dinosa glanced at her watch and said, "Sara Davies will be here in ten minutes and I'll be re-interviewing her. I'd like you," pointing to Gardner, "to accompany me," and concluded using a line she'd picked up from her fiancé, "Let's do it."

* * *

Sara Davies was escorted down the hall from the reception desk and led into 'Interview Room Two' where Dinosa and Gardner were already seated at a table. They rose when Sara entered and Dinosa said sincerely, "Ms. Davies, I speak for us all when I say how grateful we are for your coming here so soon after your mother's death and how sorry we are for your loss."

"Thank you…ah, ah, I'm sorry, but I don't remember your title Ms. Dinosa," she stuttered.

"That's quite all right. I'm Investigator Dinosa working for the District Attorney's Office, but you can call me Mary. This is Inspector Gardner with the police Homicide Division and I'm sure he won't mind if you call him Frank."

"Well, I just want this son of a bitch caught and I'll answer any questions you have and I want you to know you can call me anytime you want," Sara replied raising her chin with anger in her quivering voice.

"We appreciate that," Dinosa said and thought to herself, I like this gal.

"Let's start with her professional life. Do you know if she had any problems with anybody she worked with or did she ever mention any confrontations with patients?" Dinosa asked.

"Mom didn't discuss her work with me much. She did seem a bit tense lately and mentioned how uncomfortable this time of year was for her. She had to give year end grades and performance and recommendation reviews on her first and second year residents."

"Did she say anyone in particular that she was giving a bad review to?"

"No, I couldn't even name one of her residents."

"How about her peers or her boss, did they get along?"

"I know she enjoyed her work and she answered to Doctor Zeller and Helen Lum. Helen and her got along famously and often socialized together, going to the opera and ballet and out to dinner together. She didn't much care for Doctor Zeller. Said he was more of a politician than a doctor and he once accused her at a staff meeting of wanting his job. She told me there was no way she wanted that blowhard's job."

"How about her social life, were there any romantic relationships?"

"I'm not sure if she would tell me about any casual romance, but I know there was no one serious. There was a guy from the hospital I met a time or two, but I can't remember his name. He would accompany her to hospital social affairs, but I think their relationship was only platonic. I believe she said he worked in maintenance or something."

Mary looked at Gardner and he asked, "Ms. Davies…"

"Please call me Sara," she interrupted and remarked sweetly, looking at both of them.

"Yes Sara, would your mother ever answer her door to a stranger?"

"Nope," she answered simply and then asked Dinosa, "Is it okay if I ask you when was the last time you saw her and how she looked?"

Mary reached across the table and grasped Sara's hand in both of hers and said, "Of course, it was only a few nights ago. We just happened to arrive home at the same time and she invited me in for a nightcap and she looked great. We chatted and it was mostly about you and how proud she was of you and your studies. You know she loved you so very much."

Tears started streaming down Sara's cheeks and Dinosa got up and walked around the table and hugging Sara said, "Come on, let's go out and catch an early lunch."

* * *

"Good morning, Inspector Jones," Elena Wyeth said cheerily as Jones entered her outer office followed by Lassiter.

"Good morning, Ms. Wyeth," Jones beamed and turning toward Lassiter he added, "This is Inspector Arnold Lassiter. And please, call me Marcus."

"Okay Marcus, then please call me Elena. Ms. Lum asked me to tell you she's sorry she couldn't be here, but she had to fill in for Doctor Davies and address the senior pre-med students at Stanford University today. She did direct me to prepare the same conference room you two met in yesterday and I've scheduled the Residents to meet you there for the half hour increments that you requested. The first one should be here in about ten minutes," she declared.

She jumped up from behind her desk, walked around it and hooking her arm around Marcus' arm she lilted, "Allow me to escort you and make sure our accommodations are comfortable for you."

Jones was glad black people didn't blush and he hoped the beads of sweat forming on his forehead wouldn't give him away as they waltzed down the hall. Arriving in the conference room, Elena said "There's fresh coffee on the table over there, and a pitcher of ice water and glasses on the table. Do you need anything else?"

"Oh, no thank you, this'll be just f-fine, t-thank you," damn he thought, why am I so tongue tied?

He gawked as she walked out of the room with a slight wiggle in her knee high tight skirt.

"Not bad, not bad at all," Lassiter remarked as Elena closed the door behind her.

"Pour us a cup of coffee, will you?" Jones said as he placed his briefcase on the floor and dug out a recording device along with box labeled 'Evidence Collection Kit' and laid them on the table.

"You like your coffee like your women?" Lassiter asked.

"Okay, I'll bite, how's that?"

"Hot and black," Lassiter chuckled.

"Ha, ha…very funny," Jones retorted.

A knock at the door got their attention and a short dark skinned man with wavy black hair entered the room.

"Hello, I'm Doctor Rahal Saleem. I'm a second year Resident here," he introduced himself with an East Indian accent and continued, "But please just call me Ray."

Jones introduced himself and his partner and said, "Dr. Saleem, please take a seat."

Jones spoke in a low unthreatening tone, "We're here investigating the death of Doctor Madelyn Davies. Can you tell us about your relationship with her?"

"Oh she was a very, very good mentor and an excellent doctor in my humble opinion. I'm in my second year of general residency and plan on a specialist internship as an Obstetrician here next year. Doctor Davies has mentored and supported me for the last two years and I will miss her tremendously," Saleem replied.

"Have you ever been to her house or associated with her outside of the hospital?"

"No, except an occasional lunch in the cafeteria or the corner deli with the other Residents," Saleem said.

"Do you know anyone who might have wanted to do her harm? Can you think of anyone she had a beef with? How did she get along with the other residents?"

Saleem thought for a moment and said, "No, as far as I know, all the other Residents liked and respected her and I can't think of anyone who would want to harm her."

Jones continued asking routine questions and concluded the interview with one last question, "Would you allow me to take a DNA swab of your inner cheek? The purpose would be to eliminate you as a suspect and save both of us a lot of time."

"Not at all," Saleem said leaning forward.

After donning surgical gloves and taking a swab of the inner cheek and gums of Saleem and depositing the q-tip in a plastic evidence bag, Jones thanked and dismissed him.

A tall beautiful young woman with long wavy red hair then strutted into the room. She carried herself with confidence, but also with an air of innocence. Her name tag pinned on her white lab coat identified her as Joanne Bentley, MD, 2nd Yr. Resident.

Lassiter recognized her and before Jones could make proper introductions, and obviously smitten by her beauty, beamed, "We weren't introduced, but didn't I see you yesterday at the autopsy?"

"Why yes, Inspector Lassiter. I noticed you also. I'm working there on an intern grant as Doctor Zeller's assistant, besides my duties here. I'd like to become a Pathologist and I might want to go into Forensic Medicine and I thought the program fit in nicely with my aspirations," she answered congenially.

"Please, call me Arnie," Lassiter cooed.

Jones appeared a little annoyed and said, "Sorry to interrupt the reunion, but Doctor Bentley, I'm Inspector Marcus Jones. Please sit down."

He proceeded to ask Bentley the same questions he had asked Saleem and when it came time to ask for a mouth swab, her forehead wrinkled and she asked demurely, "I'm not considered a suspect, am I?"

"No…no, not at all," Lassiter said, "It's just routine. I doubt it will ever make it to the lab."

Jones gave Lassiter a quick look of disapproval when Bentley said, "Oh, of course. The request just surprised me."

After she departed, Jones asked the next interviewee to wait and turned to Lassiter.

"Why don't you go find Ms. Wyeth and find out where they store the camera videos and see if we can determine what Doctor Davies did the day she was murdered? I can finish the interviews."

* * *

After lunch Dinosa returned to her temporary desk in SFPD Headquarters and picked up the autopsy report from the Coroner's office and began reading. As she perused the document, she appreciated Doctor Zeller's thoroughness. The victim's stomach contents consisted of partially digested hamburger with onions, a yellow cheese, and what appeared to be mustard and catsup, along with French fries and a liquid which Dr. Zeller determined to be a carbonated cola. Based on the decomposition of the food, he estimated her time of death as two to three hours after her last meal.

She picked up her phone and dialed Lassiter.

"Hey, Dinosa here, have you picked up any of Doctor Davies' movements that day?" she asked before he had time to say hello.

"Yeah, she arrived at the clinic across the street from the hospital about 8:05 am. They don't have cameras inside the clinic, but I did see her leave at 10:30 am and cross the street to the hospital. A camera picked her up entering the side entrance to the hospital at 10:31. Another camera…"

"That's okay Lassiter, we can go over the blow by blow account later. One question, when did she eat last?" Dinosa interrupted.

"Let's see," Lassiter said and after a moment continued, "She entered the hospital cafeteria at 5:57 pm and exited at 6:19 pm. Let me find the video and I can tell you what she had to eat."

"A cheeseburger, fries and a coke," Dinosa mumbled.

"Huh..?"

"Never mind, that fits in with our time line. I'll see you later," Dinosa hung up.

Her cell phone rang and she retrieved it from the belt cradle, "Dinosa here."

"Mary, its' Margaret Johnson here, check your e-mail. The lab results just came in on the sperm DNA and they got a hit."

"Ah shit, I don't have a terminal at this desk," Dinosa groaned, "What's it say?"

"The good news is, it came back as a match to a suspect in the murder of a young woman in Burlingame one week ago. The bad news is, it doesn't match with anybody in the FBI CODIS (Combined DNA Index System) and Burlingame PD doesn't have a suspect."

"Does the report give the name of the victim and the names of the BPD investigators?" Dinosa asked excitedly.

"Yes, the name of the victim is nineteen year old Susan Darden and the case is assigned to a Detectives Sam Paulson and Josephine Morales."

"Thanks, Margaret," Dinosa said and while dialing the Burlingame PD she was thinking how the murder of this young woman could tie in with her case.

She was informed by the police operator that the two Detectives were in the field and unavailable, but her message would be passed along as soon as possible. Dinosa walked over to the adjoining cubicle and logged onto Jones' computer and googled 'Susan Darden'.

She called Gardner over and handed him a slip of paper and said "See if she's in the system."

She found a Susan Darden from Santa Clara on 'Face Book'. Her picture showed a smiling, innocent nineteen year old pretty blond girl. Her profile said she was a first year student at El Camino Junior College and she played guard on the school's basketball team. She was the eldest of three other siblings.

Dinosa wondered how a seemingly sweet young lady could be murdered by the same man that tortured, mutilated and murdered her middle-aged neighbor. Was she wrong in assuming Doctor Davies was murdered by someone she knew? Was the murder of Susan Darden just a diversion or visa versa? Who could be so diabolical they would murder an innocent young woman just to throw the cops off of his trail, and then she remembered the 'North Beach Killer'.

She rolled her chair back to the aisle and asked Gardner in the adjoining cubicle, "Anything on Susan Darden?"

"Looks like she got a speeding ticket two years ago and that's about it," Frank answered and asked, "Why, exactly, are we looking at her?"

Dinosa filled him in on her conversation with Margaret Johnson and then asked him, "What do you make of it?"

Gardner leaned his tall thin frame back in his chair and stretched his arms out and locked his fingers behind his head and mused, "Well, this sure throws a monkey wrench in our, 'it has to be someone she knows' theory."

The phone on Dinosa's temporary desk rang and she jumped up and ran over and picked it up, "Investigator Dinosa."

"Investigator, its' Detective Paulson, Burlingame PD, it looks like we have something in common."

She put the phone on speaker and motioned Gardner to come over.

"Yes, it seems we have a common murderer and we should compare notes. What can you tell us about your case?" Dinosa asked.

"Well, I'm sure you've found out her demographics by now, so the only thing I can add is she's the oldest of four children and lived at home with her two brothers and sister and her single mother and, here's the catch, our victim supplemented her income as a call girl. She advertised on 'Craig's List'.

"It appears her last whereabouts was with a client and we're trying to track down who and where they met. She was discovered in the morning, two weeks ago today, displayed naked and tied to a basketball pole in the outside playground at the 'Sisters of Learning' a Catholic elementary school in Burlingame. She was found by little school kids.

"We know that was not the murder scene, but we haven't found where she was killed yet. What can you tell us about your case?"

"Well, first of all your victim ology doesn't fit with our victim at all. She was a middle-aged doctor and we're certain she didn't supplement her income by prostituting herself. She was found displayed similar to your victim, but she was found in her own bed by her daughter."

Dinosa went on to explain the semen found in her vagina and rectum, the vaginal mutilation and the cause of death and then asked, "Does this fit with anything perpetrated against your victim?"

Paulson answered, "Yeah, everything fits, except our victim died of strangulation and her vagina was not mutilated, her right breast was excised and we haven't found it."

"We need to get together and compare notes and ideas; your place or ours?" Dinosa asked.

"I agree and we could use a road trip, how about tomorrow morning at your place?" Paulson replied.

"Sounds great, see you at 9:00 am," Dinosa said.

"Let's make that 10:00 am. The traffic's terrible at nine," Paulson said and hung up.

Dinosa looked up at Gardner and said, "Have we entered this case into the…ah…you know that FBI data base of similar crimes in the country?"

"You mean the NIPACA Coop, the National Intra Police Agency Criminal Activity Coop. Yes we have. I'll check with our FEI people and see if we got any hits," Gardner replied walking back to his desk.

"Jesus, what the fuck is it with these alphabet soup agencies. I'll bet there's an agency to come up with the acronyms for agencies," She mumbled to herself.

"What's that?" Gardner said.

"Never mind," Dinosa replied, but it gave her a thought and she picked up the phone and dialed Valerie Kane.

"Hi Val, its' Mary, I just had an idea."

Dinosa filled Kane in on the murder in Burlingame and the DNA match and how it threw their investigation into turmoil.

"So…" Kane winced, "What is it you need from me?"

"I want you to okay bringing in an outside consultant to aid the investigation," Dinosa replied, feigning boldness.

"Hah, and I want to sleep with Ellen DeGeneres," Kane groaned and added, "Whom did you have in mind to call?"

"Grub and Snoopy," Dinosa answered.

"I'm sorry Mary, but do you know how broke this City is? If there were funds and I spent them on this, they'd hang me from the nearest flag pole," Kane said.

"Valerie, you've worked with them and know how good they are. If they were given all the data surrounding this case they might at least come up with a hypothetical suspect. You could justify it by saying the time and expense saved by the PD alone would cover the cost," Dinosa begged.

"Jesus Mary, this isn't like asking mommy and daddy to spring for a new prom dress after daddy just got laid off, for cry'n out loud. I'm telling you there's just no money, zilch, nada."

"Come one Val, how about your discretionary fund?" Dinosa persisted.

"What discretionary fund? Mary, I'm telling you no," Kane stated.

"Guess I'll have to go to the prom dressed in rags then, but thanks anyhow," Dinosa whined.

Not one to give up, Dinosa picked the phone back up and dialed her fiancé, "Hi baby. Care to buy a down and out lady a beer?"

"And what do I get out of it if I do?" Ian asked.

"What kind of a girl do you think I am?"

"We've already established that. I just want to know how many beers its' going to cost me."

"How about 'Lefty's' in half an hour and you'll find out?"

"I guess I can get away. See you in thirty minutes."

* * *

CHAPTER THREE

Dinosa met Ian O'Farrell three years ago following the Barnes family when she was a Homicide Inspector with the SFPD. She was assigned as the lead inspector and it was a case she neither could or would ever get over. It would also be the first, although not the last, time she would knowingly break the law in the service of justice.

The O'Farrell family had money and lots of it. The first O'Farrell, an emigrant from Ireland, settled in the City just as the gold rush hit northern California in the late 1840's and he started a mercantile company supplying and servicing the booming population of pioneers and gold miners.

Over the years since, the family invested in real estate and divested in lucrative businesses and became a benevolent power. The eldest patriarch now is Sean O'Farrell, the father of Ian. Ian had been commissioned in the U.S. Navy and had a ten year distinguished career as a Navy Seal Commander.

His mother was a victim of the 'North Beach Killer' and following that event he resigned his commission and formed a group of fellow seal team comrades to track down his mother's murderer and bring him to justice.

Although Ian delivered the infamous serial killer to Dinosa on a silver platter, they didn't meet until after the Barnes family massacre. She discovered her former retired partner,

Chuck Chalmers, and Ian had reformed their group to chase down the people responsible for murdering the Barnes family. Insisting she be part of the team and knowing she would be partaking in illegal activity, she now realized it was the most thrilling and satisfactory chapter of her life.

In the beginning, she thought Ian was an egotistical 'John Wayne' type, but during that operation she came to find him to be a man respected by the other team members as an intelligent, fearless leader and decided to share more than just her fox hole with him.

Since their engagement, Ian had settled down to help his father manage the family business and proved to be a very good asset. He had a good mind for business and was an excellent manager of people.

Now he spotted Mary sitting alone at a table past the bar counter in the far corner of Lefty's Tavern and made his way to her. He leaned over and kissed her and said, "My budget says I can only afford two beers and a flea bag motel."

"You're so funny," Dinosa smiled and then looked away.

Ian's eyebrows furrowed and he queried, "What's the matter?"

"Ian, it's just that…it's just that I feel like a prostitute right now."

"Uh oh, why do I feel like this is going to cost me more than a couple of beers and a sleazy motel?"

"God dammit, she was such a good woman. She dedicated her life to saving lives and teaching others to do the same."

"I assume we're talking about Doctor Davies..?" he asked.

"Yes, and I don't have a clue who the hell did it."

"Well, I think you could give yourself more than a couple of days to figure it out. What can I do?"

She brought Ian up to speed on the investigation and why she needed the help of Grub and Snoopy. Snoopy, whose given name is Belinda Grant, was a former member of the SFPD's FEI (Forensic Electronic Information) Division, and Grub, whose given name is Daniel Tanaka, met when Doctor Tanaka was recruited by Ian's group to help track the 'North Beach Killer'. Grub was and still is considered the country's foremost computer engineer. The two fell in love, married and started a computer consultation firm.

"We all know they're the best, but the problem is the city can't afford them," Dinosa said with anticipation.

"So what's the problem? Call them and have them bill me," Ian responded.

Dinosa leaned across the table and hugged Ian and squealed, "Oh, you're such a jewel."

"Man, this is gonna be one expensive piece of ass. You better be worth it."

* * *

That evening she dialed the Tanaka's number and it was answered by a familiar voice, "Hi, you've reached GROOPS Consulting, May I help you?"

"Groups, what the hell is that?" Dinosa giggled.

"Oh hi, Mary, its' been a while. Actually the 'groups' is spelled G-R-O-O-P-S. We thought it would be neat to combine our two first names to call our company. It was actually my idea."

"Very original, I guess," Dinosa said, still tickled and thinking only Snoopy could come up with that.

She continued, "How are you guys doing?"

"Well, as you would say, 'busier than a one legged red neck in a shit kicking contest.' How are you and Ian doing?"

"Just fine, thank you. Listen, we'd like to hire you guys to work on a case," Dinosa said.

"Hang on Mary, I'm going to put you on the speaker phone," and then Dinosa heard her yell, "Hey honey, its Mary Dinosa! Can you get away? Mary, he's down in the kitchen cooking up something for our supper...oh, hear he is now."

"Aloha Mary, howzit?" Grub said.

"I've got a job for you if you can squeeze it in," Dinosa said.

"For you, we can squeeze it in. What is it?" Grub asked.

"It's the Doctor Madelyn Davies case. She was murdered in the apartment next to mine two nights ago. You've probably read about it."

"Yeah, but we didn't realize she was your neighbor. What can we do?" Grub asked.

"Well, I'm the lead investigator on the case and frankly I'm stumped and I need your help," Mary said solemnly.

After telling them where she was in the investigation and the dilemma the Burlingame murder had created she said, "I need you guys to do your numbers magic and give me any probable suspects or at least give me some direction. I know you've got the largest criminal data base in the world and based on my prior history with you two, if anybody can do it, you can."

"Oh yeah, this is right up our alley!" Grub said excitedly.

He followed with a series of questions and forty-five minutes later he asked, "Is there anything else you can add?"

"Not anything I can think of. Why don't you two join us for dinner tomorrow night at my place and I'll give you the case file and we can catch up on old times? And of course, anything else you need, you'll be given complete access. If you need to get into NIPCAPA I can arrange it."

"Don't worry about that, I've accessed their data base before," Grub said.

"Mary, we'd love to have dinner with you and Ian tomorrow night, what time?" Snoopy asked.

* * *

CHAPTER FOUR

"Okay Chuck, do you have an ample supply of flies," Dwight MacArthur asked his former SFPD partner as they approached the stream.

"Yeah, yeah, I might be a virgin at this fly fishing, but I'm always well-armed," Chuck Chalmers replied.

"Just checking, 'cause I know you'll be snapping feathers off of them faster than a master plucker in a chicken processing plant."

"Not as fast as you change wives," Chalmers chuckled to himself.

"What was that?" MacArthur asked.

"Never mind."

Chalmers was fulfilling a promise he had made to his wife after finally retiring. They had purchased a thirty-five foot motor home and were touring the country. Visiting his old partner and friend in Bonners Ferry, north Idaho was their final stop before driving to the coast and boarding an Alaskan cruise ship.

Yesterday they had spent the afternoon in Mack's back yard and he learned how to tie a fly to a leader and cast. Fishing was not his forte, but he figured he owed himself the opportunity to find out what the attraction was. Chalmers didn't say anything, but wondered why you couldn't catch fish with a worm and a bobber like he'd seen Mickey Rooney do in 'Huckleberry Finn'.

Chalmers stopped at the river's bank and looked around. He marveled at the natural beauty surrounding them and decided the experience justified the effort. They were in a narrow valley where the Pack River snaked lazily around boulder sized rocks and grassy banks that led to evergreen trees and steep mountains on either side. Except for the sounds of the rippling water and birds chirping the isolation was mesmerizing.

Mack tapped on his shoulder and pointed across the river to a meadow where an alerted doe stood, head up and turned, looking toward them. A small spotted fawn stood next to her nibbling unaware on the green grass shoots. Mom exhaled a little grunt, twitched her tail upright and bounded off through the meadow with her baby trailing her. Her large bushy white tail stood defiantly straight up as if to say to the interlopers, "Thanks for the disruption, ass holes," as she and her young one disappeared into the timber line.

"Wade straight out from here about a third of the way across and cast downstream. See that little eddy at the end of this ripple, try to put your fly just in front of it and let it drift into the eddy," Mack said and added, "I'll be up stream."

Chalmers, with thigh high boots on, waded out into the stream. He was about knee deep and could feel the coolness of the water on his legs through his boots. He let out some slack from the reel and then awkwardly started flailing his rod above his head, counting to himself in rhythm, "two o'clock, ten o'clock," as he had been instructed.

When he finally stopped waving his rod and halted it at three o'clock he heard a snap as the fly sailed over his head and he knew he had just denuded the artificial fly. "Shit," he mumbled.

The naked fly landed short of the eddy and immediately disappeared. He started pulling in the slack like he'd been taught, but the slack kept coming. "What the..?"

He noticed his line was coming straight toward him and then traveled between his legs. He yelled, "Mack!" as he glanced behind him and spotted his ex-partner stumbling back toward the bank, howling out of control in laughter.

"Mack, what do I do?" Chalmers pleaded.

Mack was now bent over on the bank laughing so hard he was unable to answer. Meanwhile, the now outraged and confused fish had circled back and was now heading downstream. Mack felt a tug on his boot and realized the fish had wrapped the line around his leg and was desperately trying to rid itself of the bug it'd just eaten and depart the area.

"Mack, you prick, help me, will ya!" Chalmers yelled and then started giggling as he realized his predicament and how foolish he must look.

Mack splashed out into the stream and with his net in hand passed Chalmers. About twenty feet down stream he scooped up the fish with his net and still laughing hard managed to say, "Ni...nice catch."

"You never told me what to do if I hooked one, you dick."

Later that night, gathered around the fire place at Mack's cabin, over a glass of after dinner wine, Mack shared the story of Chalmers' big catch to the delight of their wives.

"Maybe you should stick with golf," Chalmers wife Colleen laughed.

"It was a set-up, I'm telling you. This old fart was just getting even," Chalmers said and looking at Mack's wife, he asked, "Did he ever tell you why we called him 'Great Balls of Fire' when we were young men at the academy?"

"Whoa, some things are better left untold," Mack said holding up a hand and looking embarrassed.

"Oh, you hush Dwight," his wife Wanda said and smiling at Chalmers continued, "I can't wait, let's hear it."

"Well, we were all in the locker room changing into our sweats for a physical training class. Everybody new that your husband here suffered from an extreme case of jock rot and while some of the other guys diverted his attention, I smeared the inside of his jock strap with 'Heat'. It's a compound used to sooth sore muscles and like its' name implies, it burns," Chalmers stopped to snicker when his cell phone rang and looking at the caller ID he chucked, "To be continued, I should answer this."

Walking out of the room, Chalmers answered his phone, "Hey Mary, what's up?"

"Hi Chuck, how's your vacation going?"

"It's called retirement, and it is going fine. I spent today fishing with Mack."

Dinosa remembered that Chalmers always used the alibi that he was on a 'fishing' trip whenever he would disappear on 'Justice Foundation' business and she chuckled to herself knowing he'd never dipped a worm in his life.

"And how did that go?" she snickered.

"It went fine, thank you. A beautiful sixteen inch rainbow trout caught me. Now, I know you could care less about our vacation, what's on your mind?"

Dinosa related the basic facts of her latest case and finished, "Chuck I'm stymied and I'd like your input. Can I email you the case file and get your opinion?"

"Sure, but you know how much I detest these electronic communications. Why don't you Fed-Ex it overnight and I'll call you?"

He gave her MacArthur's address and said, "We'll be here for the next two days and I can review it on our drive to the coast."

He hung up and returned to the others.

"Okay, okay, finish the story," Wanda pleaded.

"Well the short of it," Chalmers picked up, "We all waited with anticipation when Mack slipped on his jock strap. We were disappointed when he showed no reaction at all. That is, until he started to put on his gym shorts. Then he kind of got a funny look on his face and then he let out a howl that would make a wolf in heat proud and started hopping around and trying to get out of his jock strap at the same time. In his confusion, instead of running through the door to the showers, he ran through the door to the adjoining women cadet's locker room. The rest of the story is history and so was born, 'Great Balls of Fire'."

The two wives were now rolling in laughter and even Mack had to chuckle and pointing at Chalmers said, "This ain't over yet."

* * *

Mary greeted Snoopy and Grub from her doorway down the hall from her apartment's elevator when they exited, "Hey guys its' great to see you."

"Come on in, its' been way too long since we've gotten together," Dinosa said, escorting the two into her home.

Hugging her hostess, Snoopy asked, "How have you two been? Have you set a date yet?"

Handing them each a glass of wine, Dinosa responded, "We're thinking maybe sometime this summer, but numb nuts, I mean Ian, seems to be dragging his feet," and changing the subject she added, "Hey Grub, why don't you join him? He's out on the lanai about to put the steaks on the bar-be-cue and I can ask Snoops about the joys of motherhood."

Grub wandered out onto the terrace and Ian greeted him with a handshake, "Hey Grub, how's it going?"

"Good, how about you?"

"Great, are you guys still living in that beautiful log cabin in the Santa Cruz Mountains? That place ought to be a national monument," Ian commented.

"Yeah, but we've added on a couple of offices and another bedroom to the rear of the house. We run our business from there. I did cut trees from the property to build the outside walls to keep the place original and now I'm being sued by the Sierra Club," Grub moaned.

"Jesus Christ, don't they have better things to do, like save some endangered swamp mosquito somewhere?" Ian responded disgustedly.

After dinner the group retired to the living quarters and sat round a coffee table in easy chairs. Dinosa served coffee and then brought out cake plates, forks, a can of ready whipped cream, and a bowl of strawberries. She returned with a plate of upside down cakes that had risen to about half the size they should have.

When Ian gave them a strange look, Dinosa said, "Yeah well, my baking skills need a little work, but what the hell, they are called strawberry 'short cakes', aren't they?"

They all laughed and Snoopy said consolingly, "They certainly are."

"By the way, before you guys leave make sure I give you a copy of the Davies' case report," Mary said.

"That won't be necessary. I hacked the SFPD system a long time ago and we're up to on the Davies' case," Grub said and looking at his watch continued, " as of two and a half hours ago."

Rolling her eyes Dinosa commented, "Of course you have."

"You know Mary, I haven't written the protocol to enter the variables of your case with all the other data yet, but just based on what I've read, I'd have to say the subject knew your victim. This Burlingame victim is either an aversion or this sick bastard decided to intentionally carry out his perversions on someone he knew," Grub said.

"That's one theory, but we need to know if this guy just started as a serial killer or if he's been at it for a time. We need a subjected profile of this guy and that's where I'm hoping you can help. I mean what kind of a prick would do this to a prostitute and turn around two week later and do the same thing to someone he knew?" Dinosa mused.

The two couples spent the rest of the evening swapping old war stories. After the Tanaka's left and Ian helped Mary clean-up, they retired to her bedroom. She couldn't keep from thinking about the case and when she shunned Ian's romantic advances he whined, "I can see our sex life won't be the same until you solve this."

Dinosa rolled over and tossed a leg across Ian and grumbled, "Oh, come over here, you big baby."

* * *

"Dammit Captain, we can't conduct a proper investigation in the fucking closet you have us in," Dinosa argued, as only Dinosa could.

She continued, "Two homicide investigators from Burlingame PD will be here in half an hour. Do you want the word to get out that SFPD would only allocate a fucking closet for a major murder investigation?"

"Dear God, why hast thou cast this Dinosa plague upon me? You know Dinosa, I thought I had gotten rid of you as a pain in my ass years ago. I must have farted too many times in Sunday school. Alright, I'll see what I can do," Homicide Chief Roger Halfhide moaned.

Fifteen minute later the Davies' case task force command center was moved to a spacious room two doors down the hall.

"Okay, until we can get more information from the Burlingame investigation, let's go over what we have," Dinosa said, standing in front of a white board with a picture of Doctor Madelyn Davies with her name written underneath and horizontal lines extending from both side of her picture that branched downward under the heading of 'Family Members and Social Friends' on one side and 'Professional Acquaintances' on the other. Extending down from the pictures center was a 'Time Line', interrupted with known times and locations of the victim ending with the estimated time of death which read, '2030 hrs. – 2230 hrs.' and the date. A line extending up from the picture titled 'Suspects' ended with a circled question mark.

"The only name here that appeared in both columns is Tom Jeffers, the Hospital Maintenance Supervisor. Marcus, did you interview him?"

"Yes and it's in my report and I taped it. His alibi for the time of the murder is pretty solid. He was attending a two day seminar at the Airport Hilton in Los Angeles at the time of death. I've verified his attendance, and it seems he was sharing his hotel room with his partner. The guy is gay. None the less, I took a swab and we should have the results anytime," Jones reported.

"Did any of the others stand out?" Dinosa asked.

"Not really, except for Doctor Harold Harris, the Medical Chief of Staff. He's a real jerk, but I don't believe the pompous ass would be physically up to the task and his alibi was confirmed by his wife that they were home at 9:00 pm watching a hot rerun of 'Doctor's Hospital' on the 'Soap Television Network'. He refused to give a swab, but if we feel it necessary, he's required to have a blood sample on hand at the hospital and we could always subpoena it," Jones said.

There was a knock at the door and it opened. A tall handsome man dressed in a sports coat and open collared white shirt held the door open for a short heavy set dark skinned woman dressed in a dark blue pants suit. Dinosa immediately wondered what they would call a man/woman 'Mutt and Jeff' team.

She stifled a snicker and extending a hand said, "You must be Detectives Morales and Paulson."

After introductions were made, Dinosa said, "Frankly, our investigation so far has netted zero suspects. We believe our suspect was known to our victim, but your case has given us pause. I hope our joint efforts can come up with some connection with your case."

"Well," Morales began, "I can tell you we've had about as much success as you have. We've interviewed her family and friends and can only conclude the perpetrator was one of her Johns. It seems she was a well-balanced, responsible, well-liked young lady and her family had no idea she advertised sexual favors for money on the internet."

"In her defense," Inspector Paulson interjected, "Her single mother thought she was working as a cocktail waitress and the family needed her supplemental income. It turns out several of her close girlfriends we interviewed were doing the same thing.

"Her mother is and has been hooked on pills and unable to work for years. The father and husband has also been out of the picture for years. It appears our victim, Susan Darden, had taken on the mother roll and since she turned nineteen she couldn't be claimed as a dependent any longer and felt the family needed the money. Since her murder, CPS has removed her three younger siblings from the home and placed them in foster homes. It's all pretty tragic."

"How about boyfriends?" Grant asked.

"Her close friends said she was seeing her Political Science teacher and had a crush on him. When we interviewed him he seemed legitimately upset and a bit guilty for having an after class relationship with a student, but was quick to tell us they hadn't slept together. We're still looking into whether or not that's true, but he has an airtight alibi and his swab came back negative," Morales said.

"Were you able to trace her 'Craig's List' soliciting johns?" Dinosaur inquired.

"Yes, well kind of. We found the last response to her ad and her return message. He contacted her via her email address in the ad and our IT people were able to recover several correspondences between the two. It appears she was supposed to meet him in two hours at the 'Sunrise Motel', room one thirty-nine, at 9:30 pm the night before her body was found. It's a sleazy motel on the El Camino Real in the prostitute corridor of town. We checked with the motel and that room was vacant that evening. The room was located in the back of the motel where the lighting is practically nonexistent. We figure he probably grabbed her there, but if he left any clues or witnesses, we haven't been able to find them," Morales replied.

"Were your IT people able to trace the source of his emails?" Gardner asked.

"Yes, it was traced back to the San Francisco Public Library, but anybody and their dog has access to about three hundred terminals without personal identification required to log on and the library people said because the terminals are connected to a single network, they can't even tell us which terminal was used. Our IT people confirmed that. The only thing we have to go on is the emails are time stamped. There's only one camera with a view of the computer complex that's the size of a high school gymnasium and there's a waiting list to get in on a first come first serve basis. Shit, we're trying to identify the men in the video, but its' almost an impossible task. We've also interviewed every library employee on duty that night with zero results," Morales said.

"Either this guy just randomly picked these two victims, which I have a hard time believing, or there's a connection we just haven't found. We know this sick bastard has to be a sexual deviant psychopath to have mutilated these women the way he did," Dinosaur said and added, "We have some people trying to profile the dick and I hope they can somehow connect them."

Gardner said, "We've tapped the FBI data base for similar crimes and should have the results soon. He isn't an amateur and my bet is this isn't his first rodeo."

"Let me save you some time," Paulson said, opening his brief case and pulling out a file and handing it to Gardner he continued, "Here you can copy our file. I've highlighted the cases that we believe have any similarities. Unfortunately there are no DNA hits."

For the next hour the group exchanged notes and theories and Dinosaur ended the meeting by saying, "I'd like to thank you both and I believe we should keep an open line of communication. Please call if you have anything to add and we'll do the same."

* * *

"Hey Mary, I'd like to thank you for not having to make idle chatter with my wife for the last six hours. Ouch... the aforementioned genteel woman and my driver just slugged me," Chalmers feigned bewilderment.

"Tell her to slug you for me," Dinosaur chuckled, "Whatsya got?"

"Well, after reading and studying the volume you sent me I've concluded there's a connection between our two victims and I think it's more than just to throw you off his trail. Doctor Davies was for sure an intended target, but if the Darden girl was a diversion, why wouldn't he have chosen an easier mark? I mean, he went to a lot of trouble to choose a call girl and leave a potential trail when he could have easily picked up a street walker to deposit his semen and then mutilate and murder her. No, I think there was more than an ulterior motive. She was somehow in his way and had to die."

"Wow Chuck, something's been bothering me and I think you've just hit it. The connection between the two victims is the murderer. Wait a second, that didn't come out right. Ah, what I meant to say is, there may be no connection between the two victims, but the suspect had a specific reason for wanting them dead," Dinosa said excitingly.

"Exactly, and this narcissistic bastard has zero regard for human life and he'll eliminate anybody in his way. He has no remorse and he will kill again. He's not like you or me. If he says, I'd like to kill that so and so son of a bitch, he does."

"Anything else?" Dinosa asked.

"Yeah, and it should be obvious to you. When I say he'll kill anybody that means anybody, including you if he feels you're getting too close. Watch your back, Dinosa. I'd hate to have to interrupt my retirement to come back here for your funeral."

"I will and don't worry. I'll make sure you're not notified," Dinosa said hanging up.

Dinosa turned toward her team gathered in their conference room for the late afternoon briefing and said, "That was retired Inspector Chuck Chalmers. I sent him a copy of the crime reports and interviews and asked him for his ideas. He's convinced there is a personal connection with the killer and both of his victims. It's a long shot, but I want you to contact everybody we've interviewed thus far and show them the name and picture of Susan Darden and ask them if they recognize her and do the same to anybody we interview in the future. Make note of their reaction no matter what their response is.

"He also reminded me that this narcissistic prick has no respect for human life and when we get close, we'll all be in danger."

Dinosa called Detective Morales and asked her to do the same with Madelyn Davies' picture and passed on the personal warning.

"Okay guys, first thing tomorrow morning I want you guys to take that picture and show it to everybody you've talked to," Dinosa said standing up and grabbing her bag before leaving.

Waiting for the elevator, her cell phone rang and she noticed it was Ian O'Farrell.

"Hi Babe, what's up?" she answered her phone.

"Ah, what's up? How about the dinner we planned tonight with each of our future parents-in-laws at 'Alioto's'?"

"Oh shit..." She had forgotten about that. It would be the first meeting of her parents and Ian's father and sister.

"Of course I didn't forget about it," she lied, glancing at her watch that read 6:05pm, "reservations at seven thirty, right?"

"Seven," he replied stifling a laugh.

Oh shit, shit, shit, she thought she'd never have time to get to her apartment, shower and change and get back to Fisherman's Wharf in time. Then she remembered she kept an evening gown with accessories for just such emergencies at her office. If she rushed she could make it.

Mustering as much confidence as she could she answered, "No problem, I'll meet you there."

Refraining from taking advantage of the dilemma he knew she was in he simply smiled to himself and replied "Okay, see you then."

She arrived at 'Alioto's' at seven fifteen and was escorted to a small private banquette room on the pier at the rear of the restaurant and after apologizing for being late she took a seat next to Ian. The west wall was a large bay window providing a view of the City's north point and the Golden Gate Bridge with the now setting sun framed between the bridges' south span.

Breaking the silence in the room, Mary's father said, "Now where was I? Oh yes, the history behind the Alioto name. They're an old San Francisco Italian family. In fact, one of the Alioto's, Joseph, was the mayor of this great city back in the sixties…"

Interrupting, Mary said, "Dad, I think the O'Farrell's are well aware of the City's history. Their family goes back well before the Alioto's hit this town."

Her father looked perplexed and recovering he blustered, "How stupid of me, I didn't realize you were those O'Farrell's. As a City Councilman I should have done my homework. Hell," he added looking at Sean O'Farrell, "your family helped build this city."

"I don't know if I'd go that far," Sean O'Farrell said modestly.

Dinosa's cell phone vibrated in her hand purse and she retrieved it. Her father grumbled, "Oh Mary, let it go the voice mail."

Looking at the caller ID, Dinosa said, "I'm sorry everybody, but I really have to take this."

She walked out of the room and stood in the hall, "Hi Grub, what do you have?"

"Hey Mary, I can't say I'm making a lot of progress with coming up with a profile for our killer, but I talked to a friend of mine. He's the head of the Genetics Research Lab at Stanford University. His name is Theodore Bernstein and you may remember him. We collaborated on locating the Johnson family and the 'GWN'."

"Yeah I vaguely remember. Bernie Rusk put you two together as I recall," Dinosa said.

"When we were working on that case he mentioned a group at the New York University was working on a project that could replicate an artists' rendition of a person from their DNA. Well, he says now they've succeeded in replicating a three dimensional image that is at least a family resemblance. They can't determine the age of the DNA donor, but they can start at twenty-five and use age enhancement to create an image at any given age," Grub reported.

"You're shitting me! What do they need from us?" Dinosa replied excited.

"I took the liberty of contacting the project's chief, a Doctor Judith McDowell and she says their work is still relatively new and not yet accepted by the scientific community or law enforcement, but here's the good news. They've just completed a couple of blind studies and the results were remarkable and they would consider our case as a beta test site," Grub said.

"What the hell does that mean? Hang on a second, will you…"

Ian was leaning through the door and said, "Mary, we're ready to order."

"Just order for me, please," Mary replied and returning to her call she said, "Okay Grub, go on."

"It means, if we agree to cooperate with them by allowing them to monitor and publish the results of their contribution to our investigation, they will agree to invest their grant money and resources," Grub explained.

"Let's do it. What do the need?" Dinosa asked.

"They need a sample of the subjects DNA and I think you should call her," Grub replied.

"Oh yes, of course. I'll call her now. What's her number?"

"Mary, it's nearly eleven o'clock on the east coast. I think I'd wait until the morning."

After taking down the phone number, Dinosa's head was spinning as she walked back into the dining room. Later that night back at her apartment, she excitedly told Ian about her conversation with Grub and his only comment was, "Does that mean if I spit on the sidewalk they can now scoop it up make my picture and arrest me? Wouldn't that invade my right to privacy?"

"Nope, your spittle would be considered abandoned property and they'd throw the book at you," Dinosa cajoled.

* * *

"Doctor Judith McDowell, please," Dinosa said into her phone sitting behind her desk in the DA's office. It was 6:03 am the following morning.

"Yes, it's Special Investigator Mary Dinosa with the San Francisco DA's office," she said after a pause.

"Investigator Dinosa, Doctor Daniel Tanaka said I might be hearing from you. It's a pleasure to talk to you. Isn't it awfully early out there?" Doctor McDowell answered.

"Yes, but Grub, I mean Doctor Tanaka, told me about your work last night and I'd like to take advantage of your generous offer," Dinosa said.

"Well, we certainly would be willing to cooperate. This would be our first official opportunity to work with a law agency, but there are certain protocols that have to be met," McDowell said.

"Such as..?" Dinosa paused.

"We did a similar replication for the NYPD a couple of months ago and the judge threw out our evidence for several reasons and it wasn't because of our science. For one, the evidence chain was broken when the DNA sample was delivered to us by a public courier service and that was before our science was even questioned at a hearing because the District Attorney had not okayed it in the first place," McDowell stated.

"I'll get our DA to authorize this today in whatever form you think is necessary and I'll have a certified evidence handler personally deliver the sample to your lab. If you have someone there authorized and certified to supervise proper evidence handling, I don't see it as a problem," Dinosa replied.

"Sounds good, I'll email you the deposition for your DA and if he signs a notarized copy you can deliver it with the DNA sample," McDowell said and after a short pause added, "Inspector Dinosa, I hope you can appreciate our position. We feel we've developed something here that will revolutionize not only criminal investigations, but also in recovering lost loved ones and reuniting families and this would be an investment for us and mean a great deal when we lobby for more funding. At this point, each replication cost about thirty thousand dollars."

"I can't promise you anything, but I may be in a position to help you down the road with foundation grant money. We are excited about your work and if this pans out, I don't think you'll have problems raising money."

"Send that deposition and I'll get back to you later this morning, and Doctor McDowell, thank you," Dinosa said hanging up.

There was a knock on her door and Valerie Kane poked her head in and said, "What are you doing here so early, trying to ruin my reputation for being the first one here?"

"Oh Val, you're just the person I wanted to see. I have a favor to ask."

"If you were the mayor, I'd be grabbing the K-Y and my ankles about now."

Later that morning, after Dinosa had the DA's authorization documents signed and notarized and called the lab with instructions to prepare a semen sample she returned to 850 Bryant Street and enter the conference room. She handed Inspector Arnold Lassiter a sealed envelope and said, "How would you like an airplane ride across the country?"

'Huh?" Lassiter looked at her dumbfounded.

"My fiancé, Ian O'Farrell, will be waiting for you at Marin County Airport in his private corporate jet. He has to travel to New York today on a business trip and has agreed to wait for you before taking off. I want you to take this envelop and pick up a DNA sample in the lab and hand deliver both items personally to a Doctor Judith McDowell, no one else. Check her credentials and have her sign for them. Nothing can break the chain of evidence. Do you understand?" Dinosa demanded.

"Yes, but I'll have to go home and pack a bag," Lassiter said, still looking dumbfounded.

"No you won't. Ian will provide a car and driver for you and after you've delivered these items he will drive you to LaGuardia Airport where a return ticket will be waiting for you at the United Airlines desk for your return flight to SFO tonight, any questions?" Dinosa replied.

"Yeah, am I allowed to ask, what's this all about?"

Dinosa gave him a quick explanation of Doctor McDowell and her group's work and ended by saying, "Arnold, don't let that semen sample out of your sight."

Lassiter walked out of the room shaking his head and commented, "Wow, what will they think of next?"

Dinosa slipped on her wind breaker, picked up her shoulder bag, left the building and drove to the Marina District where she parked at a metered space on Jefferson Street. She retrieved a beach blanket from her trunk and walked down the street to 'Joe's Fresh Crab' and bought two cracked crabs, a loaf of San Francisco Sourdough French bread and a bottle of water from the street side vendor.

She walked back toward the Aquatic Park. It was a clear late spring day and a cool gentle breeze blew in from the Bay. The subtle aroma of salt water was invigorating. She crossed Hyde Street and the Cable Car turnaround and proceeded up the lawn covered area of the park until she found a fairly secluded spot on top of a knoll. She spread out her blanket and sat her bag and lunch on it and sat herself down Indian style.

She breathed in deeply and took a moment to enjoy the weather and the view. To her left was the magnificent Golden Gate Bridge and the Bay in front of her was dotted with tall white sails that extended across the water to Angel Island and Alcatraz Island and to her south lay Treasure Island and the Bay Bridge. It was here that her former partner, Chuck Chalmers, had come to clear his mind. She had come to appreciate it for the same reason and she whispered a little thank you to him. She remembered the time he had brought her here and initiated her in the 'cracked crab and sourdough bread' ritual during a particularly difficult case and it was then she realized he had allowed her into his tight little circle and she was accepted.

She chuckled to herself as she pulled a piece of crab from its' shell and greedily stuffed it in her mouth allowing the juice to run down her chin. The first time she had grumbled about not having any napkins and Chalmers had remarked, "That's what the bread is for."

After finishing the last of the crab and mopping up her hands and her face with a piece of bread she'd torn from the round loaf, she packed up the shells in a brown bag and wrapped the remainder of the bread to save and savor later. She laid back and arranged her shoulder bag under her head and closed her eyes.

Visions of the late Madelyn Davies and her mother-like companionship and their evening chats conflicted with the scene of finding her cold nude body lying dead in her own bed. Dinosa rarely allowed her mind to wander to what the victim's last thoughts might have been. Was she sad that she would never see her beautiful daughter again and be able to see her blossom into a young lady? Would she miss her daughter's graduation and wedding day and playing with her grandchildren?

Who would want to murder this lovely woman? She had learned that the answer to 'why', when applied to a seemingly senseless murder had no explanation to a rational, sane individual. She had to get in the mind of the sick bastard to find his motivation. She remembered Chalmers' advice to look past the ugliness of the act itself and find the reason.

She drifted back to what Madelyn was thinking during her last moments. Could it have been, "Why is this person I know doing this to me?"

Did Madelyn know the answer? She must have. Then she remembered what Madelyn's daughter had said about her mother's discomfort about the Resident's reviews. Maybe she was about to fail or give a bad report on one of the Residents. Could that be motivation for him to murder her?

She made a mental note to find those reviews when her concentration was interrupted.

"DA Inspector Dinosa, can you comment on the Doctor Davies' case?"

Mary bolted upright to a sitting position and instinctively reached for her 9 mm semi-automatic pistol in her shoulder bag when she recognized the intruder. It was Reginald 'Scoop' Anderson, a reporter from the San Francisco Tribune who wrote a daily shock gossip column. He was kneeling not more than two feet from her holding out a hand held tape recorder.

He fell over backwards when Dinosa leveled the large barrel of her gun between his eyes.

"Whoa, I'm just a reporter covering a story," he stammered.

"I know who the fuck you are!" Dinosa yelled, putting the pistol back in her bag. "You little son of a bitch, you're lucky I didn't blow your brains out. How did you find me? Did you follow me?" she demanded.

"N-no, I just recognized you," he stuttered and then regaining his cockiness after she had returned the gun to her bag, he stated, "You know, there is still freedom of the press in this country."

Dinosa gathered up her blanket and trash and standing eyeball to eyeball with the little man started backing him down the hill.

"You little prick. If you ever sneak up on me like that again, I will splatter your brains all over the place. Now, get out of my area!"

That afternoon in the San Francisco Tribune evening edition under the daily column titled 'I Left My Heat in San Francisco', by Reggie 'Scoop' Jackson, appeared the following;

"Once again in our Fair City, one of San Francisco's finest, a Special Investigator from the District Attorney's Office, has denigrated our precious 'Right to Free Speech'.

This humble correspondent was assaulted at gun point by a member of the DA's Office, for simply asking a follow-up question regarding the murder investigation of the late and beloved Doctor Evelyn Davies. Out of respect to Doctor Davies and the investigation, this reporter has decided not to reveal the identification of the law enforcement officer that assailed him earlier today, but that action can only add to the fury and doubt that our City's law enforcement has the ability to react with dignity and openness in the aftermath of such a tragedy..."

Dinosa answered her phone to an angry boss, "Jesus Christ Mary, what were you thinking!"

"Whoa, what the hell are you talking about?" Mary asked, confused.

"Have you seen today's column by Reggie Jackson in the Tribune?"

When Dinosa answered negatively, Kane read her the article.

"That weasel little prick...Tony Bennett would roll over in his grave if he knew this runt was using the name of his song to call his column..."

"Tony Bennett isn't dead yet," Kane interrupted and stifled a chuckle.

"Oh, I could have sworn I read he was…" Dinosa started and then explained the events of earlier that morning.

"Well, I just got off of the phone with a very irate City Desk Editor at the Tribune and he strongly suggested you take an Anger Management course. He said his columnist had to change his britches after your little confrontation this morning," Kane said.

"Yeah, I'll take an Anger Management course when that little 'poor excuse' for a reporter takes a Journalism 101 class. Can you smooth this over, Val?"

"Probably, but Mary," Kane paused for a moment and continued, "Would you kindly take the advice your old partner gave you and learn when to keep your gun holstered and your mouth shut."

"Yes Ma'am," Dinosa said hanging up.

Dinosa turned to the two other Inspectors in the room and asked, "Did anybody have any luck with the picture of Ms. Darden?"

"Not really," Jones said and added, "Elena Wyeth, that's Helen Lum's Administrative Assistant, said she kind of looked familiar, but she couldn't recall from where."

Gardner contributed, "I showed the picture to Sara Davies, and after she looked at it for a long time she thought it might be a gal from her History course from last semester. She couldn't remember her last name but thought her first name was Linda. I checked it out and the only Linda in her History class was a Linda Blumberg and it couldn't have been our Ms. Davies."

"What school does Sara attend?" Dinosa asked.

"San Francisco State," Gardner replied.

"That's a dead end. Darden attended El Camino Junior College. Did you get any odd reactions from anyone?" Dinosa asked.

They all shook their heads no. She filled them in on the mission she had given to Lassiter and why.

"Geez, I like to think I keep up on these sorts of things, but this is the first I've heard of this kind of research," Gardner commented.

"Yeah, well like your brilliant associate Arnold Lassiter said, 'what will they come up with next'?"

She dismissed Jones and Gardner for the day and then got on the phone with Detective Morales. "Any luck with the picture?" she asked.

"Nothing, but we still have a few people to show it to. Investigator Dinosa, we're back to square one. We had this guy profiled as a younger, possibly a classmate, shy and standoffish sort. Since we've learned about your common victim, we don't know what to think," Morales said.

"I have some good news," Dinosa said and went on to tell Morales about the work of Doctor Gowen and her people and the assignment she had sent Lassiter on. She concluded, "Doctor Gowen said it would take about a week to complete their work and come up with a twenty-five year old replica of the guy. We already know he's a Caucasion and they tell me they can use age enhancement techniques to replicate his image at any age over twenty-five. It will only be a resemblance of the subject, but she says their blind studies so far are better than eye witness sketch artist's likenesses."

"That sounds great, but forgive me if I sound a little skeptical. Why haven't we heard of this technology before and are you sure they're not pulling your panties so they can get more funding?" Morales said.

"That could be true, but I have some very reliable sources that say this is legitimate. It's worth a shot and it's not coming out of our budgets."

Dinosa continued, "I suggest you continue your investigation using your current profile with an open eye. Our theory at this point is the prick is somehow known to each victim and those victims either pissed him off or he felt they were in his way and needed to be eliminated. He's a narcissistic bastard and whether or not his rape and sexual mutilation plays into his motivation, he's one smart psychopathic degenerate."

* * *

CHAPTER FIVE

Two uniformed officers with a hand truck and a Crime Scene Technologist stood outside as Jones, Gardner and Dinosa walked into the Helen Lum's outer office and Jones introduced Elena Wyeth.

"It's so nice to see you again Marcus," Elena gushed and added, "Ms. Lum is expecting you, please go right on in."

Dinosa thought she saw Grant's black face blush and chuckling to herself thought, a romance in the making or maybe already made.

The three entered Helen Lum's office and again Jones made introductions.

"Ms. Lum, I'd like to thank you for the cooperation you've extended us during our investigation and keeping with that spirit and not to ask you to compromise any hospital policy, I've come with a court order to search Doctor Davies' office and confiscate anything, with the exception of patient medical records of course, that may aid our investigation," Dinosa said attempting to use her most diplomatic tone.

Lum tilted her head with a curious look and after taking a moment to assess Dinosa said, "Why thank you, Inspector Dinosa. That is considerate of you and I appreciate you not asking me to compromise hospital policy. I'll cooperate fully, but do you mind if I summon someone from our legal staff to look over your warrant first?"

"Not at all," Dinosa replied.

Following a visit from a middle aged hospital attorney, who Dinosa thought looked like he should be wearing a curly locked wig and speak with an English accent, the group was escorted down the hall to Doctor Davies' office. It was a small windowless office, neatly decorated with nature photographs on the walls, a desk facing the door with a swivel chair behind it and two filing cabinets lining one wall. Dinosa noticed the lack of a vanity wall covered with plaques of achievement and sheep skins that donned a wall of most Doctor's offices she had been in.

Donning a pair of surgical gloves, Dinosa said, "Well, let's get started."

A computer monitor and key board sat on one side of the desk and a stack of folders were piled high on the other side. An old fashioned in and out basket sat at the front and a portrait of Sara Davies dressed in an evening gown and looking beautiful sat next to the computer.

She also noticed the door was unlocked when they entered and she asked Lum, "Did Doctor Davies always keep her office unlocked?"

"You know I don't know, but I'll make inquiries," she replied.

"I'm curious," Dinosa asked and continued, "Have you found a replacement yet for Doctor Davies?"

"No and we're desperate. Year-end evaluations and recommendations that Doctor Davies was working on are due the end of this month for review by the Medical Board before the Residents appear for their Oral Exams.

"We're taking applications for the position now, but it's doubtful we'll be able to make a decision by the deadline. The Board is meeting this afternoon to consider our course of action from here," Lum replied.

"Could you supply me with a list of applicants?" Dinosa asked.

Again, Ms. Lum tilted in her head questioningly and replied, "Ah, I suppose so."

Dinosa busied herself with disconnecting the cables from the computer while Jones and Gardner rifled through the file drawers pulling file folders out and stacking them on top of the cabinets. When they were finished purging the files, Lum thumbed through them and said, "They're doesn't seem to be any patient medical records here," she stated.

Dinosa motioned for the two uniformed officers and the CST to start bagging and stacking the file folders on the hand truck and then she sat down at the desk and was surprised to find all of the drawers unlocked. She guessed security was not a top priority for Doctor Davies, but then reasoned it wasn't like she needed to hide top secret information. In fact, she realized, their investigation had not uncovered any deep dark secrets in the life of Doctor Madelyn Davies.

She opened the middle drawer of her desk to find only office incidentals, a few pens and pencils, a box of paper clips, a box of rubber bands, a small stapler, all arranged neatly and in order. The top drawer on the right contained only a family photo album. She picked it up and paged through it. The first few pages were wedding photos showing a young Madelyn and her hansom groom she guessed was Sara's father, and the wedding party. She came upon a picture of Madelyn in a hospital bed gazing lovingly at her new born baby suckling on one of her breast.

Dinosa decided to keep the album and review it at the station and if none of the pictures were relevant to their investigation, she would return it to Sara. The middle drawer contained several plastic covered Diplomas and Certificates of Achievements and a small bag containing several colors of lipstick and eye liner and other make-up articles. She bagged and tagged these items and then opened the bottom file drawer. Behind a row of empty file folder she discovered a half pint of unopened Smirnoff Vodka. She covertly picked up the bottle and slipped it into her jacket pocket thinking, this must have been Madelyn's secret 'emergency' stash.

Dinosa stood up and said, "Ms. Lum, I'd like to thank you for your cooperation," and turning toward Jones she said, "Make an inventory list of everything we're taking and have Ms. Lum sign it and then book it into evidence at property and bring it up to our conference room where we can go over it. I'll see you back at the station."

Turning back to Lum she said, "One last thing, Ms. Lum. Did Doctor Davies have an office at the Clinic?"

"No, she would make rounds with some of the Residents and any patient information she had would be entered into the Clinic's computer. She was not the primary physician," Lum replied.

"Thank you again," Dinosa said and left the room.

At the end of the hall she spotted Lassiter engaged in conversation with a tall strikingly beautiful red haired woman dressed in a white lab coat. As she approached the two she noticed the woman's name tag read, 'Dr. Joanne Bentley' and recognized the name to be one of the Hospital's second year residents.

Dinosa approached the two and Lassiter, writing down something on his pocket pad, didn't notice her until Doctor Bentley did and tugged on the arm of his coat.

He looked over at Dinosa and with a surprised red face said, "Oh, Investigator Dinosa, I was just coming to give you guys a hand."

"I thought I gave you the day off after your late night," Dinosa queried.

"Yeah, well I did sleep in, but I thought you guys could use my help and…"

Dinosa interrupted his awkward moment and said, "As long as you're here you might as well help. Jones and Gardner are in Doctor Davies office. "I'm sure," she looked at Bentley's name tag, "Doctor Bentley here can show you the way."

"Oh, I'm sorry, Inspector Dinosa this is Doctor Joanne Bentley, she's a…"

Turning to walk away, Dinosa interrupted again and said, "I know who she is."

As Dinosa waited at the elevator she mumbled to herself, "Jesus, does the Department hire any male cops who don't think with their dicks?"

* * *

"Hey Snoops, it's Mary," Dinosa said into her phone as she relaxed on a lounge chair and stroked Tuxedo curled up on her lap in her sparsely furnished living area.

"Hi Mary, let me put you on speaker. Grub is right here beside me," Snoopy replied.

"Hello Mary, I'm sure you'll be glad to hear we uncovered two thousand, three hundred and fifteen unsolved murders in the United States going back twenty years that have some similarities to your crimes," Grub stated flatly.

"Oh, that's great. Give me the list of names and we'll get on that right away," Dinosa groaned sarcastically.

"Yes, well, we can narrow that list down to one case if we limit our search to murderers known to who have killed a Doctor and a prostitute. That case was in upstate New York about ten years ago and the cops think it was a murder for hire by the somewhat irate wife of the Doctor, but so far they haven't found the hit man to tie it to the wife.

"That does kind of substantiate my original premise that these two victims were somehow known and connected to your murderer. Our research also indicates that when you find this pervert, he'll have major sexual issues with a woman's, to put it bluntly, pussy and tits," Grub concluded.

"Madelyn Davies was not married and we haven't been able to dig up even a casual boyfriend, so we can eliminate a jealous lover," Dinosa said and then asked, "Have you broken down these similar cases geographically, like how many in California?"

"Come on Mary, you know I did. One hundred and twenty-two occurred in California, thirty-nine in Northern California and eighty-three in Southern and twenty-six of those occurred in the Bay Area. I have also arranged them in chronological order," Grub replied.

"That's a start anyway," Dinosa said and continued, "Can you deliver them in person tomorrow morning and I have another job for you."

"Sure, what else do you need?" Grub asked.

"We confiscated Madelyn's computer today and I'd like you two to conduct the forensic search on it," Dinosa said.

"We'll be there bright eyed and bushy tailed," Snoopy giggled.

Dinosa hung up her phone and found herself staring at a one eyed, one breasted pretzel-figured woman Picasso print hanging on her wall, and wondered what the hell frame of mind she was in when she purchased and hung it. Carrying Tux in one arm she walked over, unhooked it from the wall and placed its' face toward and next to the front door as a reminder to throw it out in the morning.

* * *

The muscles of Arnold Lassiter's arms, shoulders and chest bulged and his blood vessels protruded from his neck as he lay on the weight bench in the gym pumping two hundred pounds. When he reached twenty reps he rested the bar on its' support and sat up breathing hard.

"Inspector Lassiter, what a surprise seeing you here," Joanne Bentley said over her shoulder as she passed him and stopped.

"Ah, Doctor Bentley is that you?" Lassiter said between breaths.

"Oh please, call me Joanne," she replied blushing.

"And call me Arnie. I've been a member here for years, but unfortunately I haven't seen you here before," Lassiter said wiping the sweat off of his forehead with a towel.

"Oh, I signed up for a yoga class up stairs and this was my first session, but I'm thinking seriously about joining the club," she said.

"Well, allow me to give you the grand tour."

"That would be great, but I wouldn't want to interrupt your routine."

"Not a problem, I was just finishing up anyhow," Lassiter lied.

An hour and a half later on Lassiter's bed in his Fillmore Street flat, he rolled over naked with Joanne still wrapped in his arms.

"Aah Arnie, it's been so long and that was so good," she cooed.

"We need to make this a habit," he cooed back.

* * *

Marcus Jones, Frank Gardener and Mary Dinosa were gathered along with Sam Paulson and Josephine Morales in the conference room at 850 Bryant Street when Snoopy and Grub arrived.

After introducing everyone, Dinosa said, "I've invited Detectives Paulson and Morales here because I think it's important we share information of our investigations and I think what Grub and Snoopy have to say is important."

Snoopy was busy handing each officer a file folder when Grub said, "The first report is a profile of our killer. This profile is based on data we've put together from both of your cases. Its' reliability is only as good as the information you have given us. That data was entered into a program that Snoopy and I developed based upon literally tens of thousands of murder investigations both in the United States and Canada.

"This program is currently under review by the National Society of Forensic Scientists and the FBI and has not yet been approved with their stamp of approval for dissemination to law enforcement agencies, but without self-modesty, I can tell you it's the most extensive and comprehensive report of its' kind. The American Psychiatry Association has rejected it because it contains no psych evaluation data, and frankly, I think that's a good thing. I'll let you make your own conclusions.

"That said, if you skip to the last page of our report under the heading 'Profile Conclusions', you'll see that the possibility of your murderer being a male is ninety-nine per cent. There is point zero eight percent he is either gay or bi-sexual and point zero two percent our perpetrator is a woman."

Grub described the other profile characteristics in terms of probability percentages.

"For example," Grub explained, "There's a fifty percent probability that our subject has had previous psychological counseling and a two percent chance that he was institutionalized. This one is interesting. There is only a ten percent chance that he has a prior criminal record."

Grub concluded, "It's very important that you keep in mind there are exceptions to every rule and when you find this person he might not fit into any of the majority percentiles."

Dinosa held up the second report and looking at Paulson and Morales said, "This is a list of unsolved murders over the last twenty years in Northern California that, in some way, fit our murderer's profile. Grub has broken them down chronologically and by county.

"If you guys agree, I propose you take the southern peninsula, the south Bay and the east Bay and the coastal counties. We'll take San Francisco, Marin County and the rest of Northern California. I suggest we review each case from their jurisdiction crime reports and determine if any of them can be connected to our cases."

Morales looked at Paulson and then said "It sounds good to us."

"Have you guys dug up any leads?" Gardner asked.

"One of Sara's girlfriends put us on to a creepy guy from school that seemed to have a crush on Sara and when we looked into him we found he worked part time as a janitor at the Med Center, but when we compared his DNA it wasn't a match. His name is Karl Schmidt." Paulson replied.

"You know, I remember a case, I think it was in Denver or maybe Salt Lake City, some years ago where a woman saved the semen of her boyfriend in a condom and used it to set up the poor guy when she murdered another woman. Could that have been the case here?" Lassiter asked.

"I don't think this kid has brains enough to pull that off. After interviewing him we concluded his elevator doesn't go to the top floor," Morales said.

"And besides that, in the case you're referring to, upon further examination of the semen, a substance of the condom was detected in the sample which led the prosecutors to the woman. That test is now run on all samples," Dinosa said and added, "But this Karl Schmidt kid is the kind of victim association we're looking for."

"We've also identified several of Sara's johns, but we've found no connection with Davies and they've led to dead ends. It appears she was a novice in the hooking game and had only been at it a little over a month," Morales said.

"This teacher of hers', ah," Dinosa referred to her notes and continued, "William Watts, have you determined if his relationship with Ms. Darden was more than just platonic?"

"Well, he's been very cooperative and we haven't uncovered any evidence to contradict his claims," Morales replied.

"That reminds me, did you bring Susan Darden's lap top?" Dinosa asked.

Morales dug through her shoulder bag and produced a sealed paper bag containing the lap top and handed it to Dinosa. She signed the chain of evidence tag and in turn handed it to Grub and he signed the document.

"We've set you guys up in the adjoining small office where you can work," Dinosa said to Grub.

"That'll be fine. Come on Snoops, let's get on it."

After the Tanaka's left the room and Paulson and Morales had departed, Dinosa divvied up and passed out the unsolved cases Grub had provided to the three Inspectors and kept a list for herself. They all sat down in front of their computers and delved into what seemed to be the endless task of tracing down each case on their list.

An hour into their work, Jones sat up and said, "Here's an interesting case. Twelve years ago a known prostitute and junky was found dead in the 'Twilight Motel' on Lombard

Street. Her vagina had been mutilated and both of her breasts had been crudely removed with what they thought was a knife, but no spermicide was detected. Her neck had been slit and cause of death was exsanguination. The mutilation occurred post mortem. Her name was Ruth Langley."

Dinosa perked up and said, "Go on…"

"Well, it looks like the Homicide Inspectors didn't conduct a very thorough investigation. They interviewed the Motel manager and occupants of the motel and the suspected pimp, a Wilbur Finnegan…"

"I know him," Gardner interrupted, "He was one of my CIs when I worked Narcotics."

"Her criminal background," Jones continued, "showed numerous arrests for prostitution and drug possession. It seems our Inspectors didn't seem the case warranted a lot of time. Three months after the murder it was sent to Cold Case Unsolved."

"Who were the Inspectors?" Dinosa asked.

"They were Walter Murphy and Bruce Pelosi."

"That tells it all," Dinosa groaned. "I was only a rookie, but around the Department they were known as Drunk and Drunker. The following year they were unceremoniously forced into retirement."

"I'll look up her pimp. I know he was trying to clean up and go straight when he was my CI and he was working as a dishwasher at a diner on Mission Street," Gardner said.

Dinosa took in a deep breath and said, "Well, this certainly fits the M.O. of our perpetrator. You pursue your former CI and I'll try to locate Drunk and Drunker. Lassiter, find out what you can about this Ruth Langley and Jones see if you can dig up anything else on the crime investigation."

* * *

Gardner found 'Willie's Diner' on lower Mission Street not far from the Financial District. When he was a Narcotic's Officer he remembered the place as 'Richard's Diner' and it was a corner shack catering to street bums and lowlifes. It still occupied the same corner, but it was now incorporated in the corner of a high rise office building with an outside courtyard and included valet parking. He would soon learn that Wilbur Finnegan had more than just cleaned himself up.

Richard Finnegan, the original proprietor, had hired his nephew with the promise that Willard would go straight and gave him the position of head dish washer. Willard proved good to his word and became an integral asset to the business. When Richard died eight years ago, he willed the diner to his nephew.

When a big land developer came along and needed to buy the property the diner sat on in order to build a square block high rise, Willard was smart enough to hire a good lawyer and negotiated not only an absurd price for the property, but also a ninety-nine year lease for the corner spot.

Gardner smiled to himself as he entered the establishment. Old Willy had done pretty damned good for himself. It was two o'clock in the afternoon and Gardner thought it would be after the noon lunch crowd. He was wrong. Nearly every table was filled with diners. The place was decorated with baseball memorabilia and photographs mostly of Willard posed with famous Giant baseball players from yesteryear. Behind the bar above the caption 'The Three Willies' was a large picture of Willard standing between Willie Mays and Willie McCovey.

He barely recognized Willard who was sitting at a corner table with three affluent men dressed in suit and tie. He had gained several pounds and his formerly gaunt pimpled and pock marked face was now robust and hale.

As he approached their table, Willard glanced up and after a moment a wide grin crossed his lips and standing up he said, "Holey moly, is this Frank?"

Extending his hand he continued, "Fellas, this is Narco Inspector Frank Gardner, SFPD. He's one of the few people that actually showed a little faith in me when I was a rot gut whiskey drinking, crack smoking pimp. How the hell are you Frank?"

"I'm good," he said looking around, "and I see you've done pretty well for yourself too. And by the way, I'm not in Narcotics any longer, I'm in Homicide."

"Whoa, that sounds serious. What can I do for you?" Willard asked.

"Is there some place we can talk?" Gardner asked.

"Sure, in my office. Excuse me guys, I'll be back," he replied.

Gardner followed Willard and he led him through a French door, past the kitchen and down a hall to an office. The room was neatly decorated with a simple desk and a leather sofa in one corner. Photographs Gardner assumed were of family lined the walls. Willard motioned for Frank to take a seat on the sofa and he sat down behind the desk.

After some small talk about old times, Gardner turned serious and asked, "Do you remember a prostitute named Ruth Langley? She was one of your whores and she was brutally murdered in a flea bag motel on Lombard Street about twelve years ago."

Willard's head drooped and he was overcome with sadness, "Yeah," he replied, "I think about her often, believe it or not. I think I might have been in love with her at the time. She was actually a very sweet girl and just got caught up in drugs and that life style and I feel guilty for contributing to it and her death.

"My biggest regret in life is that I didn't find A.A. and clean up my own act sooner. I believe I could have helped her, but at the time I couldn't even help myself. In my prayers I've made my amends to her and I will continue to until the day I die."

He looked up and away and wiped a tear from his eye.

"Well, you might be able to help bring her some justice. We've reopened her file. Do you have any idea who might have killed her?"

"Ah Jesus, Frank, I was so messed up at the time I don't remember and can't tell you a blessed thing," Willard moaned and continued, "I always figured it was a degenerate John who just flipped out. I remember the two flat feet that were assigned to the case interviewing me and their attitude told me the case would never be solved."

"Can you tell me anything about her? Was she married or have any children? How about her parents or where she was from?"

"I believe she was originally from the Avenues and she did have a husband and a kid. A little girl I believe. Her old man had abandoned her and I never met him, but I did meet the little girl one time and I think CPS eventually took her. I know Ruth signed adoption papers, but I couldn't tell you when."

"Do you remember the little girl's name?"

Finnegan squinted his eyes trying to remember and suddenly said, "Yeah, her name was April, April Langley. I remember because Ruth told me she was named after the month she was born, April. Her mother would swear she was going straight every year on her daughter's birthday, but it only lasted until she came down from her last high."

Gardner rose, walked over and placed a hand gently on Willard's shoulder and looking him directly in the eyes, asked, "Willie, is there any chance you were the one who flipped out and did this?"

Willard covered his face with his hands and began to sob. Gardner continued to stand with his hand on Willard's shoulder until he stopped sobbing and through his hands moaned, "God, Frank, I asked myself that question a thousand times and I don't believe I did. I know I was just down the street at a dive called 'Ralph's' dinking and drugging and when the two detectives checked it out the old gal that ran the place told them I was there all night. I was really messed up and I couldn't tell you where I was all night, but I don't believe I could have done it."

"I believe you Willie, but to eliminate you I'm going to ask you for a DNA swab," Gardner said sympathetically.

"Absolutely, if I did do this, I don't deserve any of this," Willard replied, looking up and spreading his hands.

* * *

Dinosa discovered Bruce Pelosi had passed away a year ago while on a liver transplant waiting list and Walter Murphy was residing at the Laguna Honda Assisted Living Home. She drove up Market Street and onto Portola Drive until she came to the sprawling three-story assisted living complex. She paused as she parked her car and took in the marvelous view of the city skyline rising above the oak and locust trees below and to her north. She passed a group of older men playing Bocce ball on the lawn next to the paved path leading to the building's main entrance. A bridge foursome of elderly women were quarreling and playing cards under an umbrella table in a courtyard next to the entrance.

"My Lord Alice, you bid two spades," she overheard one of the ladies complaining, "That doesn't mean how many spades you have in your hand! Goodness gracious and Mary Mother of God!"

Mary chuckled to herself and prayed this would not be her fate when she was their age. After entering the front door she proceeded to the reception desk and showed her police ID to the young woman behind the counter.

"I'd like to see one of your residents, Walter Murphy," Dinosa inquired.

"Oh you must be the officer that called earlier," the young lady replied.

After Dinosa nodded yes, the young lady picked up the phone and several moments later a tall black middle aged man dressed in white pants and shirt approached them from across the foyer. The young lady handed him a slip of paper and said, "Thomas, would you escort Investigator Dinosa to see Walter Murphy, he lives in 228W."

Dinosa followed the orderly up a flight of stairs to the second floor and they started down the hall of the west wing. About halfway down the hall a double door to their left opened to a dayroom and Dinosa noticed several elderly people chatting and playing cards or board games. Double doors to their right led to a large dining room. The end of the hall met a tee and they turned right.

As they approached room 228W, Thomas stopped and said, "Ms. Dinosa, ah, Mister Murphy is what we call a difficult resident. I think it best if I accompany you into his room and stay."

Dinosa glanced through the opened door to the room and saw the back of a gray and rusty haired man sitting in a wheel chair next to his bed apparently staring out of the window.

She patted the right side of her blazer indicating she was armed and said, "Thomas, I don't think that will be necessary."

Thomas smiled and said, "Okay, I'll be right outside the door if you should need me."

Entering the room she politely said, "Excuse me Mister Murphy, I'm DA Investigator Mary Dinosa. Could we have a word?"

Murphy didn't move or acknowledge her so she moved to his side and raising her voice said, "Walter, I said…"

Murphy expertly and quickly spun his wheel chair on one wheel to face her and scowling up at her he growled menacingly, "I heard you the first time! Let me see your shield."

"Certainly," Dinosa replied calmly and produced and showed him her badge.

Attempting to sound amiable she asked, "On such a beautiful day, why aren't you outside enjoying the weather with your neighbors?"

He gave her an incredulous look and with hatred in his voice said, "What, mingle with this bunch of limp dicks and wrinkled cunts? I don't like old women or Bocce ball pushing wops. If they had a tavern and a dart board, I might leave this god forsaken room. What the hell's on your mind?"

She reached in her shoulder bag and handed him a photograph of the mutilated body of Ruth Langley. "We've reopened the murder case of Ruth Langley and as lead Inspector on that case I thought you might be able to offer me some insight."

Murphy took the picture, studied it and remarked, "Yeah, I remember this one. Shit, it happened a century ago."

"We believe there might be a connection with some recent murders we're investigating," she replied.

"Well, if they involve junkie whores, I wouldn't waste your time."

Dinosa reached down and grabbed Murphy by the lapels of his shirt and yanked him up and forward and with her face only inches from his, roared, "I don't give a fuck what you'd do! Now, if you don't answer my questions, you'll join your limp dick friends outside after I toss you from that fucking window?"

Thomas glanced around from the door and quickly stepped back out of sight with a wide grin.

"Whoa, what'ya need to know?" Murphy asked.

"How about her ex-husband, did you investigate him?" she demanded after releasing him.

"Yes and as I recall we eliminated him because he was in county lock-up at the time."

"Did she have a daughter?"

Murphy thought for a moment and after scratching his day old growth of beard, said, "Yeah, as I recall we did interview a little waif. I don't recall her name, but she was a charge of that Catholic orphanage on Polk Street."

"How come none of this is in your report?" Dinosa said shaking her head.

"She hadn't seen her mother for years and she didn't know nothing," he replied.

Hearing the double negative, she thought this guy was a double negative. She was ashamed he had served on the same police force she had taken so much pride of being a part of. She vowed to herself to talk to Valerie Kane about leading a campaign to clean up the Department of incompetent slugs like this man.

"Anything else that's not in your report?" she asked.

"Nope," he replied simply.

Dinosa turned to leave satisfied only that at least she remembered the name and location of the orphanage.

"Dinosa," Murphy called after her, "Do you think you could sneak in a pint of some Irish Rye for an old fellow flat foot?"

"Fuck you, Murphy."

Walking away from Murphy's room and down the hall, Thomas said with a smile, "Can't say I didn't warn you."

"Yeah, what a dick," she replied, "That man is an embarrassment to the City and anyone who ever wore the SFPD blue."

She dialed Jones' number as she drove down the hill on Laguna Honda Boulevard.

"Hey Marcus, where are you?"

"I'm just leaving 'Willie's Diner'. Willard Finnegan now owns the place. It's located in the lower Mission. Do you know the place?"

"Yeah and old Willard has really moved up in the world. What did he have to say?" she asked.

Jones related his interview with Willard Finnegan and finished saying, "I don't believe he had anything to do with the murder, but I got a volunteered sample of his DNA."

"So the daughter's name is April. I don't know if we're barking up the wrong tree, but I get the impression she's somehow connected to all of this. What do you think?" Dinosa mused.

"Hell, it might just be wishful thinking, but what else do we have? I get the same sense," Jones replied.

Dinosa gave him the block location on Polk Street of the orphanage and said, "Let's meet there at the front gate."

Driving to the location, she reviewed the case and tried to make sense of it. She had three victims, one murdered twelve years ago. All were women and were killed and mutilated in a similar fashion. There had to be a common connection, but what? She slammed her palm on the steering wheel and swore out loud, "Damn, maybe there is no connection!"

* * *

Jones was waiting at the gate to orphanage when Dinosa arrived and together they walked up to and through the open double door entrance. Across the foyer a young Nun sat behind a reception desk.

As they approached she looked up and asked, "May I help you?"

After identifying themselves, Dinosa said, "May we speak with the person in charge?"

"That would be Sister Shari. Let me see if she's available," the young Nun replied, picking up her phone.

A few moments passed and a pleasant looking woman in a Nun's habit appeared from a hallway and introduced herself.

"Sister Shari, we're investigating a series of murders and unfortunately it has led us here. Is there some place we can talk?" Dinosa said.

"Why don't we take a walk in the garden?" the Sister replied stoically.

"Of course," Dinosa said, thinking this is one cool lady.

She directed them to a door at the rear of the room that entered into a courtyard with cobbled paths and beautiful blooming flowers and shrubs.

"What do you need from me?" the Sister inquired as they strolled along the path.

"We're trying to locate a former charge of the orphanage. Her name was April Marie Langley and she would have been about six years old when she arrived here about twenty years ago," Dinosa said and continued, "We know she was adopted and we now have to get a hold of her. Any information you can provide would be very helpful."

"I remember little April. She was such a sweet young girl and arrived here under the most tragic of circumstances, but I hope you understand she has a right to her privacy now, and I'm bound not to give you the information you ask," Sister Shari responded.

"You know, Sister, we could get a court order," Dinosa said politely.

"Yes, I know, but perhaps I have a better idea. The girl you're interested in visits here often and volunteers her time working with the children. Why don't you leave your contact information and I'll ask her to contact you?"

"That sounds reasonable, but Sister, if I don't hear from her by tomorrow I will start the paper work," Dinosa said.

* * *

Degenerate

PART II
THE LITTLE GIRL

"Little Miss Muffet sat on her tuffet, eating her curds and whey. Along came a spider, who sat down beside her, and frightened Miss Muffet away."
A child's rhyme

CHAPTER SIX

 She was born April Marie (O'Shea) Langley on April 15, 1989 to Brian and Ruth Langley in San Francisco Children's Hospital. She weighed nine pounds, twelve ounces and was twenty-two inches long, which at the time seemed rather large, but considering her parents were both large people, it was not considered abnormal. It was a difficult twenty-one hour labor for her mother, but the result was a healthy baby girl.

 Her father, Brian, was a second year apprentice working out of the plumber's local union and her mother, Ruth, worked as a receptionist in a downtown law firm and was on a two month maternity leave. They resided in a two bedroom flat on Van Ness Avenue and were saving to purchase a home in one of the City's surrounding suburbs.

 The maternal grandparents lived on Thirty-Seventh Avenue and were almost as excited about their granddaughter's birth as the baby's parents were. Although they were not overly happy about their daughter's choice in a husband, they accepted it as inevitable and Mister O'Shea actually used his influence as a union journeyman plumber to get John into the apprenticeship program.

 John and Ruth met and fell in love attending George Washington High School where John was a three sport letterman and Ruth, one year behind John, was a cheer leader.

Had John maintained just decent grades he would have been offered a full ride scholarship to several four year universities, but he settled for a four year plumber's apprenticeship and Ruth who was an honor student and could have been accepted into any major college, elected to become a wife and mother.

April was two months old when her father decided to stop after work and have a few beers with some of his old high school buddies. Later that evening was the first time he smoked crack cocaine and it turned out to be the beginning of the end.

Ruth noticed he began spending more time out late with his friends and when she discovered their home buying funds had been spent and John had been expelled from the union, she packed up her baby, moved back into her folk's home and began divorce proceedings.

On her baby's first birthday she was informed her parents were killed in a three car accident on the Bay Shore Freeway, just a few miles from their home, returning from a long weekend of camping in the Santa Cruz Mountains.

Ruth was devastated and when she woke up to reality after a mourning period she discovered she was alone in the world with her baby and although she was the sole beneficiary of a hundred thousand dollar life insurance policy on her father and inherited a mortgage free home, her paltry income could not cover the monthly expenses of the day care center, the house insurance and property taxes, and the cost to clothe and feed herself and April. With no moral support she fell into a deep depression.

It was then that Brian appeared on her door step portraying himself as her savior. He looked disheveled and gaunt as he told her he was in out-patient rehab and about to be reinstated into the plumbers union. He seemed to be genuinely sorrowful and serious about his recovery. He convinced her to drop the divorce proceedings and began to provide her with Quaaludes to offset her depression.

Life for the next year was relatively good for Ruth. Brian on occasion would abuse alcohol and in turn verbally abuse her, but when these events happened, she would double her Quaalude usage in order to cope. Both abuses became more regular.

One evening Brian came home from work in particularly high spirits. He had successfully completed his third year of apprenticeship and was off union probation. Although he was no longer forced to attend weekly Narcotics Anonymous meetings to satisfy his union probation conditions, he would continue to do so he declared.

He suggested they celebrate the occasion, hire a baby sitter and go out for the evening. Caught up in his good mood, Ruth agreed. They went out to dinner and then to a club on Fillmore Street. She controlled her drinking with a glass of wine with dinner and nursed a cocktail at the night club. When they returned home, Brian paid the sitter while Ruth checked on their sleeping baby. She walked into the bathroom, washed down a Quaalude with a glass of water, brushed her teeth and washed off her make-up and slipped out of her dress and into a robe.

When she walked into the bedroom she found Brian bent over the dresser with a straw up his nose and inhaling a line of a white powdery substance. She realized at once it was an illegal drug and exclaimed, "Brian, what are you doing? What about your drug test?"

"Hey babe, those drug tests are over. Remember, I'm off union probation and besides this is cocaine, it's not addictive like meth is," he giddily replied.

"Here, snort a line. It'll make our love making out of this world," he smiled devilishly offering her the straw.

Not wanting to disrupt his festive mood she accepted his offer. Her nose immediately stung and she tasted acid. She jerked up and pinched her nose saying, "Wow."

He took the straw and snorted another line. "Yeah," he responded shaking his head with a grin on his face.

"Take one more hit," he encouraged her.

Already feeling giddy she followed his instructions. He grabbed her hand and led her to the bed. He was right. Their love making was fabulous, like nothing she had ever experienced. She found herself uninhibited and performing acts and in positions she would have previously been too embarrassed to participate in. When they finally drifted off to sleep she had a sense of warmth and security that she would never feel again.

The family managed to stay together for the next several years until the insurance money ran out. By that time Brian was booted from the union again and Ruth had lost her job with the law firm. Brian was arrested for petty theft breaking into cars and given a six month sentence in County lock-up. Their home was foreclosed on and Ruth found herself living in a basement studio apartment on Gough Street. April was five years old and had become a withdrawn and confused little girl.

Her mother had evolved into a full blown heroin addict and when she was sick for a fix, neglected her daughter. April would shiver in the dark corner of the filthy kitchen when her mother entertained men in her bed. When her mother was high she would fill April's head with visions of better days ahead when she would enroll her in school and dress her in newly purchased girly clothes. She would reminisce about times when April's father would run touchdowns and she would cheer him on along the sidelines. And then she would slip off into a deep sleep and leave April to fend for herself.

It was during one of her deep sleeps after entertaining one of her men friends that little April's life would be forever changed. The man entered the kitchen and found April in the *corner, sitting on the floor with her arms wrapped around her knees. She was six years old. He picked her up and carried her to the bathroom cooing, "Don't worry April, Uncle Pete's not going to hurt you."*

Once in the bathroom he dropped his pants and sat down on the commode. April turned away and attempted to leave the room when Uncle Pete grabbed her arm and forced her down in front of him. He grabbed her chin and forced her head around and said menacingly, "Now, you do what I say or I'll hurt you and your mother. Pretend it's a lolly-pop and start licking it."

It tasted sour and she began to gag. He picked her up and bent her over the bathtub and she vomited up the pork and beans she had for supper earlier that evening. Still puking and choking, she suddenly felt a sharp pain and something large enter her pee-pee. She started to scream out when a big hand covered her mouth. Her rigid body went limp as she passed out.

The next morning she walked out of the apartment and vowed never to return. She had picked up some change and a few dollar bills on the table next to her sleeping mother and boarded a City Muni-Bus on the corner that would take her to the County Family Services downtown.

At the tender age of six and a half she also learned that Mommy was a bad person and her men friends were evil. She made a promise to herself that she could make a better life for herself and that would require a diligent effort to be aware of her surroundings and resolved she would do whatever became necessary to attain that better life.

The people at County Family Services were appalled at little April's condition. She was dressed in filthy clothes and she suffered from malnutrition. She was taken to the county medical facility and after an examination it was apparent that she had indeed been raped.

Her mother was investigated by the police and Child Protective Services and she was arrested for child neglect and accessory to first degree rape. April's rapist was never caught and her mother pled guilty to lesser charges and received a six month jail sentence.

April was admitted to the children's ward at Mercy Hospital and was hooked up to an IV and fed a nutritional diet. Within a week she made remarkable progress and gained body weight and strength, but more importantly she received love and attention from the nurses and Catholic Sisters who attended to her every need. She could not remember a time when she felt so safe and free of fear.

One young Sister took particular interest in April and would spend hours sitting at her bed side brushing and braiding her long red hair and telling her what a precious, beautiful young girl she was. Once, after April snapped at her for snagging her hair with the brush, she was politely admonished, "You know, a beautiful flower will attract more butterflies than an ugly old weed."

When April was released from the hospital after a two week stay, the young Nun, Sister Sheri, took her under her wing and April was awarded custodial guardianship to the 'Sisters' of Mercy School for Girls'. She thrived in her new environment and although she was more than a year behind the other girls of her age, she quickly caught up in her studies and surpassed most of the others. She was bright and pretty and loved the attention and affection she received, ever mindful of the 'butterfly' analogy and advice.

She volunteered for every chore or detail that she was offered and became a junior care giver to the younger orphans at the school. She learned that when childless married couples would visit the ward where she worked, they would inevitably *choose one of the younger children to adopt. Now at eight years old she realized her chance at being adopted by loving parents was slim.*

When an eight month old, light skinned black boy arrived at the orphanage she devised a plan. His name was William and April took charge of his needs. She would bathe, feed him from a bottle and change his diapers and sing to him and rock him to sleep. Her attention to the little boy endeared her to the Sisters and to William. When April was in the ward she would dote attention to her new little charge and they became inseparable when she was not in class or asleep in her room.

She would talk to him and sing him songs and as he grew she taught him to walk and his first word was, "April."

One 'visitor day', a young mixed race couple toured the ward and took particular interest in little William. The white wife noticed the bond that existed between April and the little boy and at the wife's insistence, the couple adopted them both.

April's plan had worked.

* * *

CHAPTER SEVEN

The ocean going ferry ship named the 'Aurora Borealis' was being nudged up to Pier Nine in the San Francisco Bay by a couple of tug boats and Chuck and Colleen Chalmers stood at the railing looking down at the crowd gathered on the dock to greet the ship's passengers.

"There she is," Colleen cried, pointing at her daughter Jennifer who was mounted atop her boyfriend's shoulders holding up a sign that read in bold red felt pen ink, "Welcome home Mom and Pop!"

As they descended the passenger ramp, Chalmers, standing six foot-two inches tall, could see over most of the disembarking folks, and had a clear view of his daughter waving her sign. He raised his hand and pointed to a less crowded area toward the end of the pier behind the greeter's restraining rope.

When they finally met up, Jennifer was jumping with joy and slipped a brightly colored flowered lei over her father's head and hugged him. Her boyfriend, Matthew O'Farrell, did the same to Mrs. Chalmers.

"Wow," Chalmers said, "The skipper must have made a wrong turn. Are we in Hawaii?"

Hugging her mother, Jennifer rolled her eyes and giggled, "Oh Pop, you're such a nerd. The lei is a sign of welcome, duh."

"Welcome home Sir," Matthew said, dressed in his Navy blue Cadet's uniform and shaking Chalmers' hand.

"Come on Matt, we're not at the Academy now. Call me Chuck, will ya," Chalmers laughed.

"How are your mother and sister and uncle and grandfather doing?" He added.

"They're all at your place. Right about now, I imagine Grandpa and Uncle Ian are struggling to start up the bar-b-que for your coming home party," Matt replied.

After collecting their luggage the group piled into the SUV and Chuck explained that they would return tomorrow to pick up their motor home.

When they neared the Chalmers' home in the Avenues, Jennifer called ahead to alert the guests they'd be arriving soon. When they pulled into the drive way, Chalmers was surprised to see a group of their best friends. Besides the O'Farrell clan, his old partner Mary Dinosa was there along with Grub and Snoopy, and former Navy Seals from Ian's team, Steve and Nancy Cromwell, Jesse Leone and Grant Wilson.

A lump developed in Chalmers' throat when he briefly reminisced about the times shared with this group of brave young people.

Waiting in the back yard gathered around the bar-b-que pit were Solomon Goldsmith, George Armstrong and Sean O'Farrell. They all shared a sad common bond. Their wives were victims of the 'North Beach Killer'. Another bond they shared was using their combined wealth and resources that led to the capture of their wives murderer and justice in the end. They were the cornerstones of the 'Justice Foundation'.

Towards the end of the evening as the party was breaking up, Dinosa grabbed Chalmers and pulled him aside.

"Chuck, there have been some recent developments surrounding the Davies' case. Do you think we could get together tomorrow and discuss them?"

"Of course, Mary," he responded.

Dinosa laughed and said, "Excuse me, but when you used to call me by my first name I'd get all tensed. Don't ask me why. Now, for some reason, it calms and reassures me."

"Is that a good thing?" Chalmers asked with satirical innocence.

"Fuck you, Chalmers."

* * *

Chalmers entered the entrance to 850 Bryant Street and was immediately confronted by an old comrade in arms.

"Son of a bitch if it isn't Chuck Chalmers," he was greeted loudly by a big burly man with a pot belly wearing a crumpled white shirt and crooked green tie under a size too small sport jacket.

"Hey Granny, how ya doin'?" Chalmers said, shaking his hand.

It was Billy Grankowski, a veteran cop who at one time had been his partner in Vice. He had gained a few pounds, a few more gray hairs and wrinkles since he had last seen him and he wondered if he had likewise aged.

"Are you still in Vice?" he asked.

"Yep, but the Department will soon be losing one of its' finest. I put my papers in and I'm out of here at the end of the month," Granny replied, "What brings you here?"

"Just visiting a few old friends," Chalmers said and added, "The place hasn't changed much."

After exchanging a few more pleasantries, Chalmers looked at his watch and said, "It's been great seeing you again," and turning away asked, "Is Homicide still on the fourth floor?"

"Yeah, hey, let's get together for a beer sometime," Granny replied and Chalmers could see the loneliness in his eyes.

"You got it, just call me."

The elevator stopped on the second floor and John Halfhide boarded accompanied by a young lady holding a clip board. When he noticed Chalmers he looked surprised and said, "Inspector Chalmers, what brings you here?"

"Mary Dinosa invited me. She's working on a case and for some reason she wanted to talk to me about it," Chalmers replied.

"Ah, must be the Doctor Davies murder," Halfhide said and then lied, "I hope you can help her. Word is, the brass upstairs aren't too happy with her progress so far."

"I think she's a more than adequate investigator and the word I've gotten is, she's saved your butt more than once," Chalmers retorted and was relieved when the elevator doors opened and he was able to escape.

As the doors closed, Chief of Homicide John Halfhide stood stuttering, red faced with his index finger raised. Chalmers couldn't make out what he was trying to say. He found Dinosa with her team in the conference room. After handshakes and hugs from Jones and Gardner, Dinosa introduced him to Lassiter.

"Sir, it's a pleasure to meet you. At the Academy we studied some of your cases and techniques. You're somewhat of a legend around here," Lassiter beamed.

"Wow," said Chalmers, "And I thought it was just in my own mind."

"Take a seat everybody and let's bring the legend up to date," Dinosa said.

They started the briefing with a methodical and step by step accounting of the crimes and the ensuing investigation. After an hour of discussion, Chalmers commented, "It seems you've covered all your bases, but what makes you think there is a connection between your current cases and the one that happened twelve years ago? And why do you think April Langley is a person of interest?"

Gardner spoke up, "It's probably more of a gut feeling, but the cause of death and surrounding circumstances just fit. If the same perpetrator committed all three murders, it's possible that his skills have improved over the years. To go from crudely mutilating a body to concisely and almost surgically excising body parts from these women suggest he may have acquired some medical training along the way."

Dinosa added, "I have the feeling that April Langley may hold the key. We don't know where she was when her mother was murdered. We don't know where she is now for Christ's sake. She would have been twelve or thirteen when her mother was killed and there's a good chance she still doesn't know, but there's an outside chance if we can talk to her, she will know or be able to lead us to the suspect."

"It sounds like you'll be meeting her soon," Chalmers said and added, "If I were you, I'd get that subpoena in the works now."

"Do you think she won't get in touch with us after Sister Shari talks to her?" Dinosa asked.

Chalmers shrugged his shoulders and said, "I don't have the foggiest. It could be that she is now forewarned you're looking for her and who knows?"

"Shit! Why didn't I think of that?" Dinosa cried, digging through her expando file to find the subpoena.

"Here," she said, handing the documents to Lassiter, "Get these over to Judge Loess' office and tell his clerk I sent you."

"Well," Chalmers said standing up, "I've got a lunch date. I'll think about your case and get back to you," and looking at Dinosa, concluded, "In the words I heard you say when we were investigating the 'North Beach Killer' case, this fucker might be a fuckette."

Dinosa gave him a queer look and then she smiled remembering she had indeed used that expression once, early in the 'North Beach Killer' investigation when they assumed the killer was a male.

After Chalmers left, Dinosa immediately got on the phone and called Valerie Kane, "Hey, it's me. If you should receive a call from Judge Loess' office regarding a subpoena I just delivered, would you use your charm to convince him to sign it?"

"That depends on what the subpoena says," Kane answered, "Protocol says you submit that request to me and I submit it to the judge, but protocol is a three syllable word and I know it's not in your vocabulary."

Dinosa ignored the sarcasm, but did apologize and explained what was in the subpoena and the need for urgency and finished saying, "Val, you have such charm and a way with the judge Loess, I know you can sweet talk him."

"Mary, it has nothing to do with sweet talking or charm. Again, in political parlance, its' spelled t-a-c-t, another word that is not in your vocabulary," Kane said and hung up.

A half hour later Judge Loess' clerk called and said the subpoena was ready. Dinosa turned to Gardner and said, "Come on, let's go."

When they arrived at the orphanage the same young Nun was at the reception desk and Dinosa said, "We need to see Sister Shari."

"I'm sorry, but Sister Shari left a voice mail this morning that she was feeling ill and did not wish to be disturbed. She sounded terrible," the young Nun said demurely.

Dinosa furrowed her brows and said seriously, "Get her on the phone."

"But she requested not to be disturbed…"

"Sister, this is not a request, this is an order. Get her on the phone!" Dinosa roared.

"Yes Ma'am," the young Nun replied and dialed her phone. After several moments she looked up and questioningly said, "She doesn't seem to be picking up."

"Where is her residence?" Dinosa asked with urgency.

"It's annexed to the south wing," the Nun answered.

"Show us," Dinosa ordered.

When the young Nun hesitated, Dinosa repeated, "Show us now!"

They followed the Nun across the foyer and down a hallway which ended at a door and the Nun said, "This is her office and living quarters."

Dinosa pulled the Nun out of the way and behind her and knocked loudly on the door, "Sister Shari, its' Investigator Dinosa. Please answer the door."

She knocked again and when no one answered she told the young Sister to stay put and tried the door knob which was locked. Drawing her Glock from her waist holster she nodded at Gardner.

He stepped back and with one kick the door slammed open. Mary entered first and yelled, "San Francisco Police Department! If anybody's here, show yourselves with your hands in the air!"

They found themselves in a small office facing a desk with several chairs in front and another door behind it. They circled the desk and Dinosa tried the door knob. It turned and when she opened it they started down a hall and passed a bathroom on one side and a closet on the other. Dinosa stepped into the unoccupied bathroom and saw the now familiar dried blood stained rings on the floor and sink. "Ah shit," she moaned.

Gardner peered in the closet and found only several habits and some civilian clothes hanging and walking shoes on the floor. They proceeded down the hall and came to a larger room. With their guns raised they stepped into the room, Gardner covering the left that housed a small kitchen and dining table and Dinosa the right.

"Ah, no, no, no," Dinosa groaned in a guttural tone.

Gardner turned and saw the grizzly scene that had caused his partner's response. Posed on the bed below a painted portrait of the Virgin Mary, her legs spread eagle and her cotton nightgown pulled above her waist, lay Sister Shari. Blood was soaked into the bedding around her crotch and neck area and her hands were tied together and posed on her chest holding Rosary Beads.

Dinosa walked careful not to disturb anything to the head of the bed and felt for a pulse. She turned and shaking her head said, "Call it in will you? And Frank, request Margaret Johnson from CSI."

* * *

"Somebody has to know what happened to April Langley. A little six year old girl can't just disappear," Dinosa said with frustration as she paced back and forth in the conference room on Bryant Street.

"Let's look at what we've got," Jones said and continued "We know now that there's a connection between the murder of Ruth Langley and Sister Shari and that connection is the orphan April. Somebody has gone to great lengths to make sure we can't find her. The only connection we have between these murders and Doctor Davies and Susan Darden is the method and cause of deaths. Is there any chance the killer of Sister Shari left any DNA?"

"Margaret Johnson said it didn't appear she had been raped, but we won't know that until the autopsy. She did say she saw what she thought might be human tissue under her finger nails and she found what appeared to be defensive knife wounds on her hands and forearms.

"It seems our Sister put up a struggle. The finger nail scrapings have been sent to the lab and we should know in a couple of hours if they can extract any identifiable DNA," Dinosa said and added, "Arnold, the autopsy is about to begin. Would you go down and observe?"

"Sure," Lassiter said and as he got to the door he stopped and added, "Oh, by the way, I did find the evidence box on the Langley murder in 'Evidence Storage'. It only contained a photograph of her daughter, a bloody sheet, a used hypodermic needle and what was believed the murder weapon, an eight inch butcher knife. I sent everything to the lab."

After Lassiter exited the room, Dinosa commented, "That guy might make a decent Inspector after all."

"At least we have a description of our elusive Miss Langley. None of the Sisters knew her name, but she would visit the orphanage from time to time and work with the students who were having trouble with their studies. They describe her as a tall, strikingly beautiful red haired woman in her mid-twenties who was polite and seemed genuinely interested in helping the girls. I've arranged to interview those girls this evening," Gardner said.

"Let's get that picture of her daughter to Grub and see if he can do his age enhancement magic on it," Dinosa said.

"You called?" Grub said entering the room.

"Hey Tanaka, what'ya got?"

"Jesus, can you believe in this day and age, Doctor Davies' was still working with an MS-DOS operating system? When I checked with the hospital's IT people they informed me the good Doctor was averse to change and refused to upgrade," Grub said shaking his head.

"So…" Dinosa queried.

"Well, it's evident she didn't take advantage of the digital age much. She did have a 'Resident Grades and Evaluation' folder, but it was scrubbed at ten o'clock the morning after she was murdered. So far, that's all we've been able to come up with. It had been stored on the system's hard drive and a system that old didn't have much back-up memory, but we're still digging."

Dinosa's head drooped and she moaned, "Oh, that's great. Marcus, how many Residents are there?"

"There are thirteen first year and ten second year residents and I interviewed every one of them and the males volunteered DNA samples and I found no one suspicious, but I'll get started on background checks," Jones replied.

"See if you can find out where they were at ten a.m. that morning," Dinosa instructed.

Dinosa's phone rang and she picked up, "Investigator Dinosa, It's Judith Gowen, I have some good news for you. Thanks to the help of your Doctor Tanaka, we've been able to speed up the DNA recognition and replication process and we have a composite and three dimensional image of your Mister X. I just sent the encrypted attachment to Gr… I mean Doctor Tanaka."

"Wow, I'll go look at it now. Grub is just next door and thank you so much."

"We got a picture of our perp! Come on you guys," Dinosa cried motioning Jones and Gardner to follow her.

When they entered the adjoining office Grub was seated next to Snoopy and said, "I was just about to get you guys."

They all crowded around the monitor in front of Snoopy and stared at a colored picture of a twenty-five year old swarthy looking man with hazel eyes and short cropped blond hair. Snoopy clicked on an icon and the image started slowing rotating into a three dimensional view.

"Simply incredible," Jones whispered.

"Can we see the age enhancement progression?" Dinosa asked.

Snoopy clicked on another icon and started scrolling through pictures depicting the man's aging in five year increments.

Dinosa dialed Valerie Kane's number on her cell phone, "Hello Val, we got the pictures and I need your permission to release them to the media," she said attempting to stifle her enthusiasm.

"Mary, Mother of Jesus, you do know what protocol means. Yes, of course you have my permission, and Mary, send me a copy for a sneak preview."

"You got it, boss."

After hanging up, Kane said out loud, "Protocol, boss... will wonders ever cease?"

"You know Mary, as soon as these pictures hit the papers and television, the switch board here will be jammed and we'll be chasing leads for months," Jones lamented.

"If I can make a suggestion," Grub said and after Dinosa gave him a nod, he continued, "I'd man the hot line with computer literate people with some law enforcement background who will be able to enter the information into a data base. If you can prioritize the most important facts and the questions our operators should be asking, i.e. the relationship the identified person is to the caller, his approximate age, his occupation if they know, his present location, and probably the most important category would be how many times by different people this individual was identified, Snoopy and I can write the program."

"That's a great idea. We need to get the Chief to call a meeting with our Community Relation's Director, the Personnel Chief and whoever supervises the hot line," Dinosa said looking at the ceiling and then added, "We'll need the cooperation of all of the Bay Area law enforcement agencies and I need to warn Paulson and Morales. Geez, I hope we have someone here that knows how to handle this."

"All right Grub, let's get together and start on that priority list," Gardner said.

* * *

When he entered the room, Lassiter was pleasantly surprised to see Doctor Joanne Bentley, gowned up with surgical gloves on, swabbing and cleaning the dried blood from Sister Shari's naked body that lay stretched out on the cold, stainless steel autopsy table.

He felt strangely uncomfortable in a room with a naked Nun, but decided it was a result of his strict Catholic upbringing and decided for the sake of professionalism, he'd have to get used to it.

"Hey, Joanne, it's nice to see you," he said awkwardly.

She looked up and wiping a tear from the corner of her eye with her sleeve, she responded, "Oh, hi Arnie. This is so sad."

"I agree, did you know her?" he asked.

"No, but I mean, for this to happen to a woman who dedicated her life to helping others, it just shouldn't happen."

Doctor Rolf Zimmer walked into the room and said, "Well, let's get started."

He handed Joanne the scalpel and asked, "Care to do the Y cut, Doctor?"

"Of course," she replied.

She took the scalpel and started the slice across Sister Shari's sternum. Lassiter shook his head and thought to himself, this woman has professionalism.

When the autopsy was complete and Doctor Zimmer had left the room, he asked, "What time do you get off tonight? I know this great little bistro on Union Street."

"That sounds great, but I have to pull Emergency Room duty at the hospital tonight. I'm free tomorrow night though," she replied.

"That's Friday night, even better," he beamed.

After giving her the name of the restaurant and the cross streets, he practically skipped out of the autopsy room. He lost the hop in his step when he returned to the conference room and was informed the 'Resident Evaluation and Grade' file had been deleted from Doctor Davies' computer and that meant all of the hospital's Residents were now persons of interest if not suspects. That fact raised ethical questions concerning his relationship with Joanne and he realized with regret his affair with Doctor Bentley would have to be put on hold. He resolved to tell her over dinner tomorrow night and hoped she'd understand.

His thoughts were interrupted when Dinosa asked, "So what did you learn from the autopsy?"

"Oh, ah," Lassiter said referring to his notes, "the bruising and cuts on her arms were pre-mortem which suggests she did put up a struggle. Her labia had been removed, also pre-mortem which accounts for the bloody bed covers around her crotch area, but there was no conclusive evidence of rape. Cause of death was exang…assanc…"

"Exsanguination?" Dinosa volunteered.

"Yeah, that's it. She bled to death as a result of a slice across her throat that severed her carotid artery," he concluded.

"Time of death?" Dinosa asked impatiently.

"Um," he again referred to his notes, "four to five hours after she had a meal of what appeared to be sour kraut, wieners and peas."

* * *

The sun was low on the horizon as Dinosa pulled into an underground private parking space reserved for 'O'Farrell and Associates' beneath the ten story executive/living development in the Telegraph Hill District on Montgomery Street. She was looking forward to moving into the beach front home Ian and she were building in Pacifica and tired of splitting their time together between her place and Ian's penthouse suite and the hassle of traveling back and forth.

She exited the private elevator into the foyer entrance to the suite and announced herself, "Honey, I'm home."

From somewhere out of sight came the reply, "Hi Babe, I'm in my office. Why don't you pour us a glass of wine and I'll join you in a second."

As she walked through the living room she smelled the hint of garlic and as she neared the kitchen the smell blended with baked chicken. She wondered how Ian had obtained his culinary talents since he had spent the majority of his adult life as a Seal Team Commander and most of his diet consisted of MREs.

She grabbed a bottle of Merlot from the wine cooler, uncorked it and poured two glasses nearly to the brim. As she walked back across the living room toward the sliding glass entrance to the veranda and balancing the two glasses of wine and the bottle, she yelled, "I've got the wine and I'll meet you on the lanai."

Struggling she managed to get the door slid open and walked out into the crisp cool evening. She sat the bottle and one glass down on a table and stood gazing down on the street lit Embarcadero and then out to the dark waters of the bay and the string of swooping lights that identified the west span of the Oakland/San Francisco Bay Bridge. The typical ocean fog was starting to roll in and blocked her view of the Golden Gate Bridge that connected the City to Marin County.

She felt Ian's strong arms wrap around her and her tense body started to relax as she leaned back into him allowing her body to conform to his. She felt relaxed and secure and wondered if this is what they wrote about in those romantic novels.

"So how was your day?" he asked gently.

She turned around, pressed her palms on his chest and whined, "Jesus Ian, you had to go and ruin a perfect moment."

"I'm sorry," he replied, "Why don't you set the table and light the candles and I'll check the oven and serve us dinner out here and we can talk about it."

"Fine," she said abruptly.

Ignoring her, he went inside and to the kitchen. When he returned several minutes later with a bowl of salad and a plate of the entrée, the table was set and the candles were lit. He sat the food in front of Dinosa and disappeared only to return a minute later with a platter of sizzling baked chicken breasts.

"Bon Appetite," he said taking a seat across from her.

"Ian, I'm sorry, its' just this case has me all tied up in knots and I should know better than to bring it home," she apologized.

"I'm a big boy and I can live with it. If it'll do any good, would you like to talk about it?" he said.

She took a sip of wine and between bites of the heavenly meal she related everything about the case and where they were in the investigation. Almost an hour later, she pushed back from the table and piling the empty dishes she said, "You really out did yourself this time. That was dee-lishish."

Ian started to stand when she continued, "No, please stay put. I'll just put these dishes in the washer and be back in a second."

She returned with another bottle of wine and poured them each a glass and asked, "So, what do you think?"

"Well, my investigating skills are lacking, but since you asked, has it crossed your mind that your mystery man has an accomplice, or rather, could your mystery man be an accomplice and doing the bidding of someone else, maybe a woman?" Ian replied.

"You know, and not in those words, Chuck Chalmers had a similar comment. Do you think a woman could have so much control over a man he'd commit these terrible crimes for her?" she mused.

Ian simply shrugged his shoulders and said, "You know I'd kill for you."

* * *

The following morning, Dinosa arrived at 850 Bryant Street at a little past seven a.m. The entire team was already assembled in the conference room and busy on the phones.

"Geez, how early do I have to get here to beat you guys?" she asked rhetorically.

Gardner hung up his phone and said, "We all got calls from Halfhide this morning at five a.m. and were ordered here. The response to publishing our person of interest last night has come close to jamming up our phone lines and people are complaining about being put on hold for more than twenty minutes. Surrounding jurisdictions are complaining about the same thing."

"Holy shit," Dinosa steamed, "Everybody was warned about this and it's not the first time we've published pictures of persons of interest for Christ's sake."

"Well, you can tell that to the Captain. He requested to see you when you arrived. They're waiting in the Chief's office for you," Gardner replied.

"They?" Dinosa questioned.

Gardner just shrugged and Dinosa mumbled, "Ah shit," as she walked out of the conference room.

When she arrived at the Chief of Police's office on the fifth floor she was directed to an adjoining conference room and when she entered she was greeted by the Chief Madelyn Keene, Homicide Chief Captain John Halfhide, and someone she recognized was from the Mayor's office but couldn't remember his name.

"Investigator Dinosa, good to see you and thank you for joining us. I'm not sure if you've met Vice-Mayor Vincent Alioto," Keene said.

Extending her hand and with a bit of relief, she lied, "Of course, how are you Vincent?"

"I'm fine, but the Mayor's office is concerned with the negative response we're getting from our citizens and the City's image after the release of these pictures to the media. Can you give us any assurances that this action will lead to solving this case?"

It's spelled t-a-c-t Dinosa reminded herself and hoped her red face and bulging temples would not give away the rage building inside her.

She took a deep breath and remaining outwardly calm, she replied, "I can't give you any assurances," she started and looking at Keene and then Halfhide she continued, "but I can tell you that this likeness of our yet to be identified suspect is real and we felt for the safety of our citizens and the possibility that someone could provide a lead that could identify this person, would outweigh any negative effects. I believe all of you were given a heads up before we released the images."

She wondered if what she'd just said made any sense and then remembered she was speaking to a room full of politicians and hoped they believed what her father had always said, "If you can't buy them with brilliance, buffalo them with bull shit," or something like that.

"I would ask the naysayers, what would you do if one of the victims was your daughter? We're investigating a serial murderer and this action is more than justifiable," she concluded and then added, "I believe our team would better serve the investigation by following up on the leads and not manning the phones."

"I agree, but I'm going to ask you to continue to provide me with updated reports of the investigation," Keene said.

"Captain Halfhide can provide that information for you. I'm sure Inspector Lassiter has provided him with daily updates," Dinosa said.

Keene glanced at Halfhide who gave her a red faced nod and Dinosa thought, gotcha!

She was dismissed and almost skipped out of the room. As she entered the elevator, she patted herself on the back for her performance; she was sure Valerie Kane would have approved. Returning to the fourth floor she was followed into the conference room by Grub carrying several dozen sheets of computer print outs.

"Okay everybody, this is a list of prioritized called-in suspects starting at the top with the most calls received. I've also emailed each of you this list." Grub said, plopping the stack on a table.

"Okay, let's ignore the incoming phone calls for a while and get started on these leads. Keep in mind with all the convoluted intel we've gathered so far, we may be looking for a conspiracy involving more than just one suspect," Dinosa said.

Answering her cell phone she said, "Dinosa here...Yes... It is...Thank you," and hanging up she pumped her fist and yelled, "Yes!"

Everyone looked questioningly at her and she said, "That was the lab. DNA results confirm the skin cells found under Sister Shari's finger nails are a match to our suspect. There has to be a connection between the orphan girl and her mother's murder twelve years ago and our three recent victims."

"All right, we'll start on this list with phone interviews," she said, opening her email and continued, "I see the first name is 'Roger Hancock, age 45' and twelve people have called in to say the pictures look like him. I'll take this one, Jones you take the next one, Gardner the third and Lassiter the fourth, and we'll rotate in that order. Got it?"

They all nodded and Dinosa scanned the list of call-in names that claimed Roger Hancock looked like the suspect. On a scale of one to five how the caller rated Hancock as their suspect, five being the most confident, she started with the only name that gave him a five rating. She picked up the phone and dialed the number of Giselle Hancock who claimed to be his niece.

Before she could finish dialing, Grub interrupted her and said, "I didn't include the name of one person who received by far the most call-ins. His name is Robert Hale, and most of the callers gave him a five, but there's a snag."

Dinosa looked at him bewildered and asked, "And that snag is..?"

"Most of the callers said he died almost a week before Susan Darden. I looked into it and they were right. His name is or was Robert Hale and he was a Muni Bus driver and was knifed to death on the job and robbed. The crime is assigned to Inspectors John McVey and Leroy Davidson here in Homicide."

"How many people recognized him?" Dinosa asked.

"Forty-two," he replied.

"Ah cripes, could this get any more screwy?" she moaned, "Get me that list, will you?"

She finished dialing Giselle Hancock's number, but couldn't get Robert Hales' name out of her head. It turned out Miss Hancock claimed her uncle had raped her. Dinosa asked if she had reported the crime and was told she had and nothing was being done about it. Dinosa asked if she could come in with a picture of her uncle and made an appointment for later that day.

She looked up the crime report which stated the rape allegation investigation was dropped by SVU when it was confirmed that the Uncle was in Italy on a business trip when the alleged rape took place. A rape kit also tested negative the victim had even been raped.

The next number on the 'Roger Hancock' list was Giselle's mother who confirmed her brother-in-law had been out of the country for the past two weeks and that her daughter suffered from 'mental problems'. Dinosa crossed him off her list.

Florence Valstead, the chief clerk in Homicide, stuck her head in the door and said, "Investigator Dinosa, I'm sorry, but there are two women at my desk insisting they talk to you. The lady introduced herself as Marjorie Hale and the other one is her daughter Bridgette."

"Hale?" Dinosa mused and added, "That's okay Flo, I'll see them."

She met the two women at Valstead's desk and after introducing herself she invited them to the first small conference room her team was assigned. She estimated the woman to be about forty-five years old and her mousy looking daughter to be in her mid-twenties.

Sitting down at the table, Dinosa said sincerely, "I assume you must be Robert Hale's wife and his daughter. You have our deepest condolences."

"So you know about my husband and how he died? We haven't been able to get any answers from your people. When we saw his pictures on the news last night and then again in the papers this morning, we thought maybe you could help us," Mrs. Hale said, looking longingly at Dinosa and wiping her nose with a Kleenex.

"I'm so sorry Mrs. Hale, but the person's picture and the man we're trying to locate is alive," Mary replied consolingly.

Marjorie Hale lowered and shook her head.

"Show her the pictures, Mom," her daughter said.

She reached in her purse and pulled out a stack of pictures and handed them to Dinosa. They were age progressive photographs of Robert Hale. As she thumbed through the pictures her curiosity and eyes widened.

"The last one was taken about a month before he was murdered," the daughter said.

"Would you wait here a moment, please?" Dinosa said standing up.

Walking next door and joining her team she was amazed at the likeness of Mr. Hale and their suspect. She sat down in front of her computer terminal and called up the age progressive images and compared them to the photographs she had spread out before her.

"Holy shit," she exclaimed, "Take a look at this."

The rest of the team gathered around and behind her. The resemblance of the pictures of Robert Hale as he aged, were almost identical to the monitor display of their suspect.

"Oh my God, that's our guy!" Lassiter blurted out.

"Yeah, except he's been dead for over a month," Dinosa moaned.

"The resemblance is amazing and almost too coincidental. Maybe he has a twin," Jones contributed.

"Let's get McVey and Davidson in here," Dinosa said, standing up and leaving the room to join Mrs. Hale and her daughter.

Attempting to sound consoling, she said, "Marjorie and Bridgette, I'm so glad you came in. You've been very helpful and I promise you I will personally look into the death of your husband and father and I will keep you updated."

"Oh, thank you so much Detective Dinosa. We do appreciate that. I want you to know that my husband was a simple man, but he was a good husband and father and he didn't deserve this," Mrs. Hale replied.

As the two were leaving the room, Dinosa asked, "One more question. Is there any chance your husband was a twin?"

Mrs. Hale looked confused and answered, "I don't think so. He was adopted as a baby and never knew his natural parents."

Dinosa wanted to yell, "Ah Shit, not another orphan!" but instead said, "Thank you again."

She walked back to the conference room, slumped in her chair and sighed, "Did we get ahold of McVey and Davidson?"

"Yeah" Gardner replied, "Their in the field and on their way in, should be here in about fifteen, twenty minutes."

"Lassiter, dig up the crime report on Robert Hale and find out what they have on the victim's background. It turns out he was another orphan," Dinosa said and as an afterthought added, "Jesus Christ, is there any responsible mothers and fathers left in the world?"

* * *

PART III
THE ADOLESCENT GIRL

"The difference between perseverance and obstinacy is that one comes from a strong will and the other from a strong won't." Henry Ward Beecher

CHAPTER EIGHT

April came to realize her good fortune was a result of her plan and always portraying herself as the 'beautiful butterfly'. It was more than good fortune that brought her to a gorgeous home in the Piedmont Hills and a life as the fairy princess. Her new parents were not only loving, but they were also financially well off and able to offer her the best of all worlds.

Her mother was an Obstetrician and Gynecologist with a thriving practice and her father was a very successful Senior Computer Engineer with a dot com company in Silicon Valley. Shortly after her adoption she requested a change of her given name to Irene Angelia and it was promptly granted.

She continued to lavish love and attention on her now new brother William because she realized it was in her best interest to do so. As they grew older, little 'Billy' became more dependent on his big sister and their parents marveled at the loving bond between the two.

Another unforeseen tragic event would challenge Irene to amend her plan. When she was twelve years old her mother's sister and brother-in-law were killed in a plane crash that took the lives of all on board. The couple had a thirteen year old daughter and with her aunt as her only surviving family member, Irene's parents adopted her.

After considerable self-debate, Irene decided her best course of action would be to accept her new sister and be the 'beautiful butterfly'. That persona suited her well and she sometimes fooled herself that it was really true. Then she would have the recurring nightmare of Uncle Pete bending her over the bathtub. She would wake with cold sweats and the feeling she was back in that basement studio apartment shivering in the kitchen corner. When she would snap back to reality she would berate herself for allowing those thoughts to interfere with her plan. It had served her well and she became more resolved that nothing or anyone would ever send her back to being that scared little girl.

For her adoptive parents, life revolved around their immediate family. Other than one living older sister of her adoptive father who lived on the east coast, her family became the nuclei of their lives' with few outside intruders. Summer holidays were spent traveling abroad and day trips to museums and other family outings. Winter holidays were filled with ski vacations to various resorts around the world.

Irene saw little importance or need to build friendships outside of her family circle and did her best to instill that feeling in her siblings. She took her new fragile sister under her wing and although she was nearly a year younger, her older sister willingly yielded her will to Irene.

As the family grew and prospered and Irene came to feel comfortable and protected, two thoughts and fears were never very far from her mind. The first was her fear and resolve to never again return to where she came from and the second was her fear of what would happen when she would be expected to leave this comfort zone and face the real world on her own.

Irene had to constantly remind herself the end justified the means and if she diligently adhered to her plan her fears would eventually fade away.

* * *

CHAPTER NINE

Inspectors John McVey and Leroy Davidson walked into the conference room and were greeted by Dinosa. McVey she remembered from her days in Homicide as a good cop and investigator. She thought he must be at least fifty years old and he now appeared to have earned every year. Davidson was probably in his early thirties and she had been informed he only had a little more than one year in Homicide.

She explained to the two why they had been requested to see them and were showed the photograph comparisons.

McVey looked at his partner and remarked, "Well, I must say he's a dead ringer for our Mr. Hale, but," he concluded looking at Dinosa, "Mr. Hale is a dead ringer."

The comment elicited several chuckles, but was accepted by Dinosa with a stern look.

"I apologize for the snide remark," McVey said, "It's just the fact that he's been dead for over a month and unless you believe in ghosts or zombies, he couldn't be your doer."

"Do you have any suspects in your case?" Dinosa asked, biting her tongue.

"Not really. We believe the guy was probably homeless and drunk or high on drugs when he shivved Mr. Hale. He operated the Nineteen Polk route and it happened at the end of his route at Van Ness and Twelfth. It was his last trip and occurred approximately twenty-two hundred hours. The dumb bastard thought he could get the fare collection box, but the dub shit didn't realize it was idiot proof. There was evidence that the box had been tampered with, but we got no prints. He stuck the driver five times. One of the stabs partially severed his Aorta and he bled out on the floor of his bus.

"The bus driver's empty wallet with cash and a credit card missing was found next to his body and his pockets had been gone through. According to his wife, Mr. Hale never carried more than twenty dollars on him. Ironically, his keychain with the key that would have removed the fare box was also found next to his wallet. Oh yeah, his wedding band was also missing."

"Any witnesses?" Jones asked.

"We located an elderly lady that got off the bus at Market Street, a couple of blocks from the end of the route. She told us she remembered only one other passenger on the bus when she exited. She described him only as a creepy, dirty looking street person. She thought he was white but that was about all. She couldn't even give our sketch artist enough to make a drawing," McVey replied and added, "Two officers in a cruiser became suspicious when they passed the bus for a second time still parked at the same corner and checking out the bus they found the deceased."

"What did the background check on Mr. Hale dig up?"

"He was forty-five and apparently happily married for twenty-six years. He left a twenty-four year old daughter who works as a dispatcher for Checker Cabs and a twenty-one year old son who is a Junior attending Cal Poly. Mr. Hale was adopted as a baby and is survived by his adoptive mother who resides in an assisted living home. His adoptive father is deceased," McVey answered.

"We haven't found anyone that might have had a personal grudge against Mr. Hale," Davidson added.

"Did you locate his natural mother or father?" Dinosa asked.

McVey exhaled heavily and stated, "We didn't feel the need to waste our resources and go there. Listen Mary, I've been at this job long enough to know where our time is better spent. We've canvassed the homeless areas and local pawn shops and we've passed out our cards, but unless this guy uses the credit card, tries to pawn the ring, starts bragging to his buddy or I get a late night visit from God Almighty himself, we're not going to solve this one.

"Listen, we appreciate that you have your own case to investigate, but I really think your barking up the wrong tree here and if you have no more questions, we have a murder investigation on Potrero Hill that we can solve."

"You're probably right," Dinosa conceded, "Thanks for coming in."

After McVey and Davidson left, Dinosa sighed and said, "Okay guys, it's time for a reality check and a team meeting."

Grub and Snoopy were summoned from the next room and they all sat down around the table in the center of the room. Dinosa started, "McVey thinks we're chasing our tails and brought up a good point about prioritizing our time and resources. I'd like to hear what's on your minds."

Jones was the first to speak, "I have to say I'm a little skeptical about the work we've received from NYU. We're spending a lot of time here looking for a suspect based on a science that hasn't been accepted by any other law enforcement agency in the country. It seems to me we've been diverted from our primary lead. The most direct motive to the murder of Doctor Davies is who erased the 'Evaluation and Grade' file from her computer? I still haven't completed my background checks of the hospital's Residents."

"The other connection," Gardner said, "is Sister Shari and the orphan lady only she could identify. Why is a Nun murdered after she presumably informed this mystery lady we were looking for her?"

"I would never presume to tell you how to prioritize your time and resources, but I can tell you Doctor Gowen's work is legitimate. My friend, Doctor Teddy Bernstein, who is the nation's leading researcher in the field of Genetics, is so impressed with her work he's taking a months' sabbatical to join and work with her and her people," Grub said.

"I've seen blind studies of their work and I can assure you that their reproductions are remarkable. I can tell you this reproduction will look like the guy you're after," Snoopy added.

Dinosa looked at Grub and asked, "Have you had any luck retrieving Davies' scrubbed file?"

"I'm afraid not. Unfortunately her operating system was so archaic there is zero chance of retrieving that file. It debunks the theory that what's in cyberspace stays in cyberspace."

Dinosa stroked her chin and finally said, "Okay, Marcus, go back to your background checks and Frank, see if you can find out who our mystery lady is. Arnie, you and I will continue to follow up on the call-ins."

As the group broke up later that afternoon, Dinosa said, "Hey, today is Friday. Tonight I want you all to go home and relax. We're going to take the week end off and I want everybody to relax, enjoy yourselves and come Monday morning I want everybody fresh and ready to solve this fucking thing."

* * *

Lassiter sat at a table for two in the corner of the small dining room inside 'Bistro Les Femme' strumming his fingers. He was experiencing mixed emotions. He was looking forward to seeing his new flame and a woman he sensed felt the same about him, but also wondered how she would accept his, 'we have to put our relationship on hold', proposal.

He noticed her immediately when she entered. Her long red hair was swirled up and pinned above her neck and she wore a simple peasant's dress hemmed just above her knees and a white cotton shawl draped her shoulders. He thought she was beautiful and didn't notice the eyes of the other men in the room follow her as she walked across the room.

He stood to greet her and after a brief hug, he pulled her chair out saying, "Joanne, you look stunning."

"After seeing me mostly in scrubs and a lab coat, I would imagine anything would look good," she replied and added, "This place is great. I love the Continental flavor. If the food here is close to being as good as the ambiance and company, it'll be a bonus."

They made small talk as they ate and after desert was served, Joanne asked, "Why do I get the sense you have something to tell me?"

He thought, oh boy here we go and started nervously, "Actually I have and, ah, it has to do with the case I'm working on…"

"Do you mean the murder of Doctor Davies?" she interrupted.

"Yes and a matter of ethics. You see, our relationship could be misconstrued as a conflict of interest," he stuttered.

"Does that mean I'm a suspect?" she asked incredulously.

"No, I mean yes, no I mean no. I mean of course I don't consider you a suspect. That would be ludicrous. It's just that we discovered some files have been erased from Doctor Davies' computer and that puts all the Residents on the suspect list. God, I hope you understand," he pleaded.

Joanne looked away and Lassiter thought he had lost her when she looked back at him and reached across the table and laid her hand on his and said, "Arnold, of course I understand."

His heart leapt with joy and grabbing her hand with both of his, he exalted, "Oh thank God, I was so worried you wouldn't. I hope when this is over we can pick up where we left off."

"Well, I was hoping," she smiled wickedly, "that since we're already together tonight, we could prolong this session at your place, off the record of course, Inspector Lassiter. I promise to make it extra special."

* * *

The cool brisk late autumn breeze was refreshing as Dinosa pulled her suitcase across the sidewalk to Ian's awaiting SUV, double parked in the street outside of her loft. Over her right shoulder she toted a pair of snow skis.

"Ian, where did I find you?" she said handing him her skis and tossing her suitcase in the back of the vehicle.

"If I remember correctly, it was on that Tenderloin corner in the red light district," Ian replied with a laugh as he clamped her skies next to his on the roof top carrier.

"Ha, ha, and you were the worst john I had that night," she chuckled, "Seriously, I told the team to take this weekend off and relax and you come up with a trip to Steve and Nancy's ski resort. How did you know this is exactly what I needed?"

"John's intuition I guess," he replied.

* * *

Frank Gardner pulled into his driveway at his home in Daly City and depressed the remote to open the door of his attached garage and parked. He picked up the bucket of fried chicken next to him and barely exited the car when his six year old daughter attacked him from the door to the house, yelling through two missing front teeth, "Daddy, Daddy, I did all my alphabet today and the teacher gave me a gold star!"

Picking her up with his free arm, he said, "That's great honey."

He carried her inside and was greeted by his three year old boy who ran up and threw his arms around his leg and said, "Oh boy, kensucky fwied chewkin."

Sitting the bucket down on the kitchen counter he mocked, "Okay, okay, unhand me you pirates. Where's your mother?"

"The pirate's mother is right here," his wife said, coming down the hall carrying their six month old baby son.

"So, how was your day?" he asked patting her on her behind and leaning down to kiss her.

"I finished papering the baby's room today," she said proudly.

"Well, let's have a look," he replied.

They walked back down the hall to the baby's room and walked in. "Wow, it looks great," he commented and added, "Whoever said a mother's work is never done."

"Speaking of work, I can't wait to get back and I didn't think I'd ever say that," she said.

Gardner's wife, Samantha, worked as a paralegal for a law firm in town and had been on a six month semi maternity leave. She still spent several billable hours a day doing research from her office in their home.

"Hey, I've got the entire weekend off and I'm supposed to relax. Why don't we get a baby sitter after we feed the kids and go out. Maybe we can catch a movie or something," he said.

"Oh Frank, that sounds nice, but I'm pooped and I'm still a little uneasy about leaving junior with a sitter. Why don't we rent a Net Flix and cuddle on the couch. We can put the kids down early and cuddle in the bedroom," she cooed.

"Sounds good to me," he replied as he patted her on the behind again.

* * *

Jones was fantasizing about Elena Wyeth as he negotiated the traffic on the Bay Bridge and was wondering if he could build up the courage to ask her out and if she'd accept after the investigation was over. It seemed to him that she had gone out of her way to let him know she was single and unattached. Was that a tell, he wondered?

He snapped back to reality when the traffic slowed to a stop as he took the East Fourteenth Street exit. He pushed the 'on' button of his hands free and voice activated phone and said, "Dial Freddy."

When a woman picked up he said, "Hi Tasha, its Marcus. Is Freddy there?"

"Oh hi Frank, yeah he's got his jersey on and rare'n to go," she replied.

"That's great. Tell him I'll be there in about ten maybe fifteen minutes."

Marcus was a 'Big Brother' to eleven year old Freddie. He became associated with the "Big Brother' group five years ago when he was working in Vice. One of his CIs was a hooker who was working the lower Mission District and he made the mistake of getting personally involved with her. The relationship was strictly platonic, but he soon found himself trying to get her out of her circumstances and then he met her six year old son Freddy.

He got Tasha a job as a receptionist working for a commercial developer who was a friend of his in Oakland and she cleaned herself up. The problem was Freddie didn't have a father and when Marcus looked into the 'Big Brother' association he was persuaded to become one. He didn't regret his decision as he watched little Freddie transform from a ghetto kid with little hope to a confident young citizen.

He had two tickets to the Warrior basketball game that evening and looked forward to taking his little brother.

* * *

Monday morning at exactly eight a.m. Dinosa walked into Homicide and was greeted by Florence Valstead, "Good morning Mary," and skewing her face she chuckled and added, "Is the raccoon look the latest fashion?"

She was referring to Dinosa's dark red facial complexion except for the white circles surrounding her eyes some referred to as the skier's face.

Dinosa shrugged and replied, "I spent the weekend skiing and I guess my attempt to blend my make-up didn't work so well."

"Nope," Florence responded bluntly, "and by the way I put the updated call-in list on your desk that Grub sent in earlier. He called and said he and Snoopy would be working from their home today and if you needed him you could reach him there."

Mary had retrieved a compact from her purse and was looking at herself in the mirror and grumbled, "Ugh, you're right and thanks."

She walked across the room and down a hall and into the conference room. Jones was the only one there, sitting at his desk and when he noticed Dinosa he cried, "Ah, hide the women and children! It's the attack of the giant she raccoon!"

"Ha, ha," she sneered, "Where's your partner?"

"He was going to interview some more of the Sisters and children at the orphanage," he replied.

She sat down at her desk and picked up the updated list of call-ins. Ten people were added to the 'Robert Hale' list. She scanned the caller's data and decided to ignore these. She went on to the next name and picked up the phone.

An hour later she hung up her phone, looked around and asked Jones, "Do you know where Arnold is? It's after nine already."

"I haven't seen nor heard from him," Jones answered.

She picked up her phone and punched in Valstead's desk, "Florence, has Inspector Lassiter called in?"

After a moment she hung up and pondered, "Florence said she hasn't heard from him," and then an ugly and frightening thought occurred to her and with a quaking voice she said, "Get Lassiter's address and have two uniforms meet us at his apartment. I'll get my car and meet you out front."

She jumped up and instinctively patted her belt to ensure she had her sidearm and hustled out of the room. As she impatiently waited for the elevator to descend to the garage parking lot level she thought about the profile Grub and Snoopy had put together about the subject being a psychotic murderer, allowing no one or anything to get in his way and a similar warning from Chuck Chalmers to be careful.

Jones jumped in beside Dinosa who was double parked outside the entrance to 850 Bryant Street. With the grill blue and red lights flashing and the blue light inside the rear window doing the same, he barely got the door shut when she floored the accelerator and peeled out into traffic. When she reached Market Street she narrowly missed a streetcar as she fish tailed making a left hand turn. When she forced a cab up onto the sidewalk and passed the irate driver flipping her the finger she glanced at Jones who said nothing, but looked up toward the heavens and crossed himself.

When they reached Lassiter's apartment on Filbert Street, a police cruiser was already double parked out front. Two uniforms were standing on the sidewalk outside of the building's entrance. Dinosa pulled up and parked behind the cruiser.

They both jumped out of the car and the two uniforms followed them into the building. Lassiter resided in the second floor walk-up flat and when they reached his door, Dinosa pounded on it. When no one answered, she pounded louder and yelled, "Lassiter, open the fucking door!"

On the first floor an elderly women opened her door, stepped outside and yelled up, "What's all the racket?"

Dinosa turned around, leaned over the railing and looked down the stairway at the elderly woman and said, "Sorry ma'am. We're with the Police Department. Have you seen or heard from Arnold Lassiter?"

"I haven't seen him all weekend which is unusual. He generally stops by to see if I need anything from the grocery store or the pharmacy every other day or so."

Dinosa looked at the larger of the two uniforms and said, "Bust it in."

"Are you sure we don't need…" the cop started.

"Now, dammit!" Dinosa ordered.

Looking confused, he peered questioningly at his partner who wore two stripes on his sleeve. After a nod from his superior, the larger cop took a step back and with a kick that would make Bruce Lee proud, the door jamb splintered and the door flew open.

Dinosa, with her pistol drawn, was the first to enter the apartment. Jones was behind her and the two uniforms followed.

"Lassiter, its' Investigator Dinosa and Inspector Jones and two uniform Police Officers! Show yourself!"

The apartment was a typical San Francisco flat with the front door opening to a long hall and an open living room to their left with a view from the front windows of the street. The first door on their left as they passed the empty living room and maneuvered down the hall was a bathroom with the door open. Jones stepped in and flung open the curtains to an empty shower stall.

They proceeded down the hall to another open door to a small vacated bedroom. The hall ended with a kitchen on their left and a dining room in front of them. Dinosa motioned for the two uniforms to clear the kitchen and she and Jones stepped into the dining room. They approached a closed door located on the left wall and she said, "This will be the master bedroom."

She tried the knob and discovered it was unlocked. Nodding at Jones she flung the door open and lowered her weapon with outstretched arms. They were met with a cool breeze that carried with it the familiar stench of death.

Laying naked spread eagle, face up with his arms and legs tied to corresponding bed posts was the dead muscular body of Inspector Arnold Lassiter. His neck had been sliced from ear to ear and his head lay in blood soaked sheets and a black sock protruded from his mouth. The laced curtains billowed in from an open window to the alley below.

"Ah shit, shit, shit," Dinosa groaned, "Oh Arnie, how did you let this happen to you?"

Jones took a step forward and Dinosa put out an arm to stop him and said, "No, he's obviously dead. We don't want to disturb the scene. Wait here and call Margaret Jonson and get her team out here."

She noticed drops of blood leading from the bed to the opened door of the adjoining bathroom and careful not to disturb anything she walked across the room and looked in. It was empty, but she noticed the dried bloody water stains in and around the sink. She also detected the faint aroma of a woman's perfume.

* * *

On the drive back to police headquarters, Jones asked, "Could our perp be a transvestite?"

"That's certainly a possibility, but I think it's a woman with a very willing accomplice and I think that woman is April Langley. She's probably changed her identity, but when we find her we'll find our doer. I think she's a sicko who also murdered her own mother over twelve years ago."

"That would have been when she was only twelve or thirteen?" Jones mused.

"Yeah, and what's your point?" Dinosa asked rhetorically.

Jones simply tilted his head and shrugged.

She dropped Jones off at 840 Bryant Street and said, "Keep digging into those background checks. I have to go see my boss."

When she reached Valerie Kane's office she knocked and opened the door. Kane was on the phone and covering the mouth piece with a hand, she said surprisingly, "You knocked first?"

Cutting off her caller she said, "Yes Marty, I'll give it some thought. Good-bye."

Shaking her head and chuckling she said, "That was Marty Goldbrick, I mean Goldsteen. He heads up a political organizing committee and tells me they want me to run for Mayor. Hey, you could come along as my personal security."

"Sorry Val, I love you dearly, but I wouldn't take a bullet for you," Dinosa replied.

Kane laughed and with a raised eye brow asked, "What's on your mind?"

"I need a court order to exhume the body of one Robert Hale. He was a Muni bus driver and was murdered a little over a month ago."

"Oookay..." Kane started dubiously, "And will we get any argument from his survivors?"

"I don't know, but I've got a gut feeling he's somehow involved in the Davies' case," Dinosa argued.

"Uh, the last time I checked, 'Dinosa's got a gut feeling' didn't carry a lot of weight with the judge," Kane replied with a crooked smile and added, "You know we could save a bunch of time if we got the family's permission."

"Okay, okay, so I never tried to have a body exhumed," an embarrassed Dinosa said.

"I think you've been watching too much television," and Kane went on to explain the necessary steps to have a body exhumed.

Leaving the room Dinosa said, "Thanks and I'll get right on getting the wife to sign off, if you'll get the paper work started."

"You're, ah, welcome," Kane said to nobody.

Back at 850 Bryant Street, Dinosa plopped down in her chair and asked Jones, "How are the background checks going?"

"Well, I was concentrating on the male Residents until you convinced me with your conspiracy theory that our suspect is a woman. The only male Resident that raised a red flag was this Doctor Rahal Saleem. He's here from India on a student visa and if he flunked his Internship he would probably lose his visa and be shipped home. I checked his college transcripts and it looks like he barely qualified to take his boards. I just started looking into the females," Jones said.

"Good," Dinosa said and added, "I've never known of a Hindu serial murderer."

"How'd it go with your boss?" Jones asked.

"I convinced her to get a subpoena to exhume Robert Hale's body. I need his DNA…Oh, that reminds me I need to call his wife," she replied.

"If all you need is his DNA, just call the Coroner's Office. They routinely keep a DNA sample on file of all murder victims," Jones commented.

"You gotta be shit'n me," Dinosa said picking up her phone.

"Hey Val, "she exclaimed, "Put a hold on that subpoena, something's come up."

"What the hell is going on…" Kane said into a dead phone.

Turning toward Jones Dinosa said, "We need to look into Lassiter's love life."

* * *

PART IV
THE WOMAN

I am woman, hear me roar in numbers too big to ignore,
and I know too much to go back and pretend 'cause I've heard it all before,
and I've been there on the floor, no one's gonna keep me down again.
I am Woman.
I am Invincible.
I am Strong.
I am Woman.

Lyrics from the song 'I am Woman', written and sung by Helen Reddy

CHAPTER TEN

 Irene and her sister were in their Junior year enrolled at the University of California Los Angeles, both taking pre-med courses and were home for Spring break when yet another family tragedy occurred. Irene was home alone early in the evening on a Saturday when the doorbell rang.

 She opened the door to two uniformed police officers who identified themselves as Piedmont Police. The female officer asked if they could come in and after sitting Irene down in the living room, she informed her that there had been a terrible automobile accident involving her family and her parents and they believed her brother and sister were dead. They asked her if she had any close relatives or friends or maybe a neighbor she could call to be with her.
 Irene covered her face with her hands and lowered her head and wept. She simply nodded her head and asked when and where it happened. They informed her they were not sure when the accident happened, but a pair of hikers only several miles from her home discovered the car at the bottom of a ravine off Skyline Boulevard. They believed her father failed to negotiate a hairpin turn. There were no witnesses to the accident.

When Irene asked when she could see them she was asked if she could come down to the County Morgue in the morning to identify them. She replied she would and after the female officer gave her a card and was assured someone would be coming to be with Irene they departed.

Under the headline 'Victims of Fatal Accident Identified' in the next day's local newspaper the article read... 'The fatalities of an accident that occurred on Skyline Boulevard sometime yesterday afternoon have been identified as family members, Garret Harley Bentley and his wife Wanda Delores Bentley and two of their children, fifteen year old William Jonathan and Irene Angelia. They are survived by daughter, Joanne Marie Bentley.'

Her plan was working perfectly.

* * *

Michael Lassiter, Arnold's father and also a retired Captain of the San Francisco Police Department and former Deputy Chief of Police, was dressed in his police blues. After entering the Homicide Squad room, he was escorted to the conference room and approached Dinosa who was on the phone.

She glanced up and noticing the Captain's bars on his shoulder and name tag, she said into her phone, "Thanks Margaret for putting a rush on this and please let me know when you get the results."

She stood up and offering him her hand she said, "I'm so sorry, Sir. It was a shock and a loss for all of us here."

He stood with his cap under his left arm and extended his right arm and shook hands with Dinosa. His eyes were blood shot and his lips quivered slightly and she was surprised when he said in a strong voice, "Investigator Dinosa, my son spoke very highly of you and your reputation, I know, is highly regarded around here. I know you can't comment, even to me, on an ongoing investigation so I won't ask. I just felt the need to meet the people he worked with and will be responsible for bringing this animal to justice. I'm here as Arnold's father and to answer any questions you might have."

She introduced him to Marcus Jones and said, "I appreciate that Sir, and please have a seat."

She continued and asked tactfully, "Can you tell me if Arnold had any girlfriends or romantic relationships."

"He didn't talk much to me about his personal life, but his mother might know more about that sort of thing. I know he was serious about a college sweetheart when he attended the Academy several years ago, but I believe she got cold feet when he proposed to her. I know they split up shortly after that and I don't believe they're seeing each other anymore."

Jones spoke up, "Sir, can you think of anybody that had a beef with your son and might be capable of doing this?"

Shaking his head, Lassiter answered, "I've racked my brain and I can't think of a soul. He only had a couple of close friends, mostly from the gym, but he was basically a gentle giant. I sometimes wondered why he wanted to become a cop. I'll give you the names and contact information of his friends."

"Captain Lassiter," Dinosa said respectfully, "When would be a good time to talk to your wife?"

"Right now she's pretty upset. She collapsed when we received the news and she's now in the company of a bunch of family and friends and our younger son. You're welcome to drop by the house anytime, but I'm not sure what shape she'll be in," he responded.

He stood up and said, "I really should be getting back to her if you're done with me."

"Again, Sir, accept our sincere condolences and I'll call you later to set up a time to see your wife," Dinosa replied.

At the door Lassiter stopped, turned around and said, "Investigator Dinosa, you asked about a romantic connection. I know I shouldn't ask, but does that mean your suspect might be a woman?"

Dinosa simply smiled, shrugged and winked at him.

After Lassiter left, Dinosa plopped down and exhaled with a blow, "Wow," she said, "That's the one thing about this job I could gladly do without."

Jones was looking at his computer monitor and said, "I've been looking into one of the hospital's female residents. Her name is Doctor Joanne Bentley. When I interviewed her she said she was interested in pursuing a career in Pathology, but I notice on her Residency application she said she wanted to be a Pediatrician. I also noticed Arnold nearly tripped over his dick whenever he was around her."

"Is she a tall, red headed beauty that also works in the Coroner's office?" Dinosa asked perking up.

Jones tapped a few keys on his computer and after a moment said, "Yep."

"I think I saw him actually trip over his pecker. What else do you have on her?"

"Well, when she was a Junior at UCLA she lost her entire family in a car accident and she was granted a hardship transfer to UC Berkeley where she received her bachelor's degree in Child Psychology. She's living right now at a student's dormitory at the hospital, but she lists her permanent address as a home in Piedmont."

"Let's get her in here," Dinosa ordered.

Her phone rang and she picked up.

"Mary, it's Margaret, we've got a definite DNA match with John Hale and your mystery man."

"Damn, I knew it. How come it wasn't discovered in our initial search?" Dinosa asked.

"Well, from what the lab tells me it just goes into the victim's crime file to confirm his identification, but never goes to the criminal data base," Johnson replied.

Hanging up, she turned toward Jones and rubbing her hands together she said, "Marcus, it is starting to come together now."

"How do we tie in Joanne Bentley with John Hale?" Jones asked.

"Let's get her in here. I have to make a call," Dinosa said picking up her phone.

PART V
THE SHE-DEVIL

I always get what I aim for
And your heart and soul, is what I aim for.
Whatever Lola wants Lola get.

Lyrics from 'Whatever Lola Wants Lola Gets' sung by Sarah Vaughan, words and lyrics by Richard Adler and Jerry Ross

CHAPTER ELEVEN

Joanne Bentley was satisfied that all the people she had eliminated had been the culmination of extensive research and planning. Her only regret was killing that whore that was sleeping with the college professor who professed to be in love with her. Even though the hooker had it coming, she had allowed her passion to overrule her self-discipline. She lamented that the deadly sin of jealousy could ruin her destiny and she resolved not to allow that to happen again and then promptly dumped the academic.

Her whore junkie mother had to die because she had to cut the ties to her past. No one could ever know this sad chapter of her life and she knew the nightmares would eventually stop. She reconciled the genital mutilation as a diversion to any investigation, but occasionally wondered if it also satisfied her need for revenge.

The murders of her family had been planned for years. It was simply a matter of logistics and convenience. Assuming her sister's identity after their deaths would forever cut all ties to her past and assure her future financial security. She actually smiled as she drilled the small hole in the family car brake fluid lining.

Doctor Madelyn Davies was about to crush her plan of following in her adoptive mother's footsteps and becoming a successful Pediatrician. She had no intention of spending her life peering through a microscope in a lab someplace as a nerdy Pathologist. Her 'beautiful butterfly' persona had not worked on the self-righteous bitch. She stood in the way of her plan and Joanne took pride while pulling off the perfect murder. She knew they would connect the good Doctor's murder with the whore in Burlingame and they would be spinning their tails forever.

When Sister Sarah told her the Inspectors wanted to talk to her, she knew her inevitable death had to occur now. She had served her purpose.

That's when that naïve, stupid, muscle head of a cop got in the way. She had originally seduced him so she could stay close to the investigation. That last night in his apartment, after she learned from him that his associates didn't know about their tryst, she realized they must never know. It didn't take much convincing for him to allow her to tie him up for a going away night of sexual debauchery. She giggled at the irony.

Now she would use the recent demise of Doctor Davies as her reason for transferring her Residency status to a program at another teaching hospital. The loss of her mentor as well as a good friend would certainly justify her request for a transfer.

She knew she had to remain strong and resolved. She realized from her pillow talk with Arnold that she would now be considered a suspect, if only a distant one. She knew the evidence she had left at the scenes would lead them to a male suspect.

Her plan continued to work flawlessly and she would continue with her 'beautiful butterfly' image. She had not had her nightmare of Uncle Pete for years now.

* * *

CHAPTER TWELVE

"Make mine a double," Dinosa said as she removed her hip holster and laid her sidearm on the table next to bottom of the spiral staircase.

Ian, standing dressed in Bermuda shorts, an aloha shirt and open toed sandals, continued to pour from the carafe of burgundy. "That kind of a day, huh?"

"Actually it was a great day, we solved the Davies case," Dinosa replied.

"Wow, that calls for a little extra. Come here and tell me all about it," he said topping off the cocktail glasses.

She joined him at the bar and pulled up a stool and took a long gulp from the glass of whiskey he handed her.

"Honey, this has to be one of the most bazaar cases I've ever been involved with. It makes the planning by George Spinella when he murdered nine innocent women in an attempt to cover-up killing his wife, look like a piggy bank robbery," she started.

An hour later, Ian kissed her and pouring again from burgundy carafe he said, "That's quite a story. What do you think prompted her actions?"

"That's one for the psych books. I know she had a terrible young childhood. I've had thoughts of what I would have done if I was the investigator of her mother's murder and knew the circumstances."

"And..?" Ian said with anticipation.

"Well, would I turn a blind eye and say justice has been done and if I had, would Madelyn and the others still be dead?" she sighed.

Ian walked around behind her and massaging her neck said, "And when ifs and buts are candy and nuts, we'll all have a merry Christmas."

She lowered her head and purred. After a few relaxing moments, she swiveled her stool around and placing her hands on the front of his shoulders, she said seriously, "Ian, if you could describe me in one word, what would that be?"

"I couldn't describe you with one word," he answered with a laugh.

"Come on, I'm serious," she replied.

He thought for a moment and then said, "Industrialist, I'd describe you as an industrialist."

"What the hell does that mean?" she winced.

"You said one word," and seeing that was not going to satisfy her he continued, "Okay, if a pessimist says the cup is half empty, and an optimist says it's half full, an industrialist finds a way to fill it."

Dinosa tilted her head, smiled and mused, "I kind of like that."

"So, where does the investigation go from here?" Ian asked.

"Well, after I've interviewed Joanne Brantley tomorrow morning, I have to meet with Val and whomever she's appointing to prosecute the crime and lay out our case," she answered.

The outside door buzzer rang and Ian said, "I thought you'd like something from the country of your roots, so I ordered pizza delivered."

"Oh Ian, you're so sweet. Tomorrow night I'm going to prepare sauerkraut and wieners and call it Irish cuisine."

* * *

"Good morning Doctor Bentley. My name is Mary Dinosa and I'm an Investigator with the San Francisco District Attorney's Office. I believe you've already met SFPD Homicide Inspector Marcus Jones," Dinosa said politely inside Interview room one on the fourth floor at 850 Bryant Street.

"It's nice to meet you Investigator Dinosa and it' good to see you again Inspector Jones," Bentley replied demurely.

"You need to know that you're not under arrest and you are free not to answer any of our questions and you are free to leave at any time," Dinosa stated.

"Goodness, that sounds like I'm some sort of a suspect?" Bentley said in the form of a question.

"Right now, almost everyone connected with Doctor Davies is considered a suspect," Dinosa lied.

"I understand," Bentley replied with a smile.

"Can you account for your time the night Doctor Davies was murdered?" Dinosa asked.

Bentley looked incredulously at Jones and then back at Dinosa and said, "I already told Inspector Jones, I was in my campus living quarters studying."

"Are you acquainted with a young lady named Susan Darden?"

Bentley took a moment and answered, "I don't believe so."

"How about Robert Haley?"

"No."

"How about Sister Shari?" Dinosa asked in rapid succession.

"No."

"How about Ruth Langley?"

"No."

"Joanne, or should I call you April, how about April Marie O'Shea Langley?"

"Ooooh, please go away," the nightmare was happening again. *She curled her legs beneath her on the chair and curled up with her head and ears buried on her knees and rocking back and forth she wailed as if she were a six year old little girl again, "Oh Mommy, you're s'posed to protect me. Why Mommy, why?"*

As she continued to wail, Dinosa stood up and with a tear in her eye and said, "Irene Angelia Bentley, you're under arrest. You have the right to remain silent, you have the right..."

"Ah shit, Marcus will you get someone up here from Forensic Psychology?" Dinosa said sadly with a sigh.

She left the room walking briskly and not looking at anyone. Down the hall she entered the restroom and hid in a stall where she sat down on the commode and buried her head in her hands and wept.

* * *

Colleen Chalmers answered the knock at her door and upon opening it, said, "Mary, how nice to see you. Please come in."

"Hi Colleen, I hate to bother you with no warning," Dinosa apologized.

"Oh don't be silly. You know you're always welcome to visit. Follow me, the Lord is in the study," Colleen replied.

Hearing their conversation through the open door to the study across the front room, Chalmers said, "Who goes there?"

"Tis the Lady Mary come to visit, me Lord," Colleen chuckled.

"Ah, a loyal subject she is, you may enter fair Lady Mary," Chalmers replied with grandeur.

As she entered the room, Chalmers swiveled his chair around and motioned Mary to have a seat on the leather couch across from him.

"Hey Chuck, what're you up to?" she asked anxiously.

"I'm just checking out the route for our next trip. We're leaving in a week for Phoenix. Colleen has a sister and brother-in-law living there and he loves to play golf. We'll probably stay there about a month and take the slow road to Florida. We're going to take the old Route Sixty-Six. You know, Ed Byrnes from 'Kooky, Kooky, lend me your comb', or was that Seventy-Seven Sunset Street'?"

"Huh?" she looked bewildered.

"Never mind, what was I thinking? What's on your mind?" Chalmers said with a chuckle.

"Well I, ah…" Dinosa paused.

"Wow, I've never seen you tongue tied before. Just spit it out for crying out loud," he said leaning forward and acknowledging her anguish.

"Okay, my Lord. You know then, how hard it is for me to ask for advice. Actually I don't need your advice…I just need an ear," her voice tailed off.

Chalmers, realizing the seriousness in her tone, said, "Okay Mary, I'm all ears."

"We found the murderer of Doctor Madelyn Davies and you were right about the killer having a connection with all the other victims, but it's more complicated than that."

She retrieved a file folder from her bag and asked if they could move to the living room where they both sat down on the sofa and she opened the file on the coffee table. She started laying out the case as she planned to do for Valerie Kane later that day.

She concluded saying, "You were right, she did have an accomplice. It was the DNA from a dead bus driver."

When she had finished her presentation, Chalmers asked, "So what's the problem? It appears to me that you've got an open and shut case."

"I know that," she sounded exasperated and continued, "It's just I feel so bad for April, or should I say Joanne, or should I say Irene. I'm trying to reconcile those feelings with the fact that she's a cold blooded serial murderer.

"You told me once when we were breaking the law we swore to uphold, that we individually had to satisfy ourselves that the end justified the means. I was able to do that then, but this is different," she said sadly.

"I think I understand what you're saying," Chalmers said softly and continued with the same tone, "I once had a similar conflict of feelings. It was during my first year in Homicide and I was partnered with an old veteran, Timmy Connors. We were investigating the murder of a father of three that occurred in the Marina District. It turned out he was sexually molesting his three year old daughter and was murdered by his brother-in-law."

"I had to deal with one side of me wanting to give the guy a hug and a medal and the other side that compelled me to cuff him and take him in."

"How did you deal with it?" she asked.

"Well, old Timmy was a recovering alcoholic and when he detected my dilemma he gave me a prayer that helped and I've used it a lot since. You know I still think about that case every once in a while and I suppose I'll take it to my grave. It comes with the job, I guess."

"What was the prayer?" she asked.

"God, give me the serenity to accept the things I cannot change, the courage to change the things I can and the wisdom to know the difference, Amen," Chalmers said solemnly.

He continued, "You know Mary, our job is not to be the judge, jury or executioner. We don't even know if our job ends with justice. We are merely investigators trying to do the best we can."

Mary gathered her papers together, put the folder back in her bag and then hugged Chalmers, saying, "Thanks Chuck, thank you so much."

Before exiting the front door she turned and said, "What happened to the guy?"

"He pled guilty to manslaughter and got fifteen to twenty-five. He got out about ten years ago and I looked him up and he forgave me."

She hugged him again and yelled her good-bye to Colleen over his shoulder, turned and feeling better she walked to her car.

* * *

Dinosa walked confidently into the conference room in the District Attorney's Department at City Hall. Already sitting at the table were Valerie Kane and one of her most hardnosed and successful Deputy Prosecutors, Jonah Stein. They greeted each other and Dinosa produced the file from her bag and laid it on the table.

She started, "To understand this case we have to go back to when April Langley was six and a half years old and the day that pathetic little girl walked alone into the offices of Family Services. The investigation into her circumstances revealed she had been brutally raped. She was under nourished and her clothing was dirty and soiled. Her mother was discovered in a filthy studio apartment, high on drugs and entertaining a John. She had no idea of where her daughter was and couldn't remember when she had last seen her or where she might be. She thought she might be at the playground park down the street. In fact, at that time she had been under Child Protective Services for over six hours.

"Little April was subsequently granted custody to the 'Sisters of Mercy' school for girls, an orphanage on Polk Street, and under the direct supervision of Sister Shari. She seemed to flourish there and several years later she was adopted.

"Unfortunately, after we visited Sister Shari, she refused to divulge her identity and citing disclosure laws, she couldn't tell us anything about her adoptive parents. Using poor judgment, I allowed her twenty-four hours to inform April we were looking for her and to arrange a meeting. Understand at that time we didn't know her name and did not consider her a suspect. In retrospect, I should have immediately procured a court order and subpoenaed the records. When we returned the following day, we found Sister Shari murdered in her living quarters. DNA extracted from finger nail scrapings were matched to the same murderer of Doctor Davies and the young woman from Burlingame, Susan Darden."

She paused, sighed, took a deep breath and continued, "That DNA did not match anybody in the system and our joint investigation with Burlingame PD, turned up no suspects.

"That's when a good friend and consultant on this case, Doctor Daniel Tanaka, told us about a group at New York City University that were making great strides in reproducing facial images from DNA samples. We sent them a sample of our suspect and they supplied us with the pictures we've all seen in the papers and on TV.

"The overwhelming response we got from the public was the pictures resembled a Municipal bus driver, Robert Hale, who had been murdered on his route a week before our first victim was murdered. We concluded it was a dead end, but it kept eating at me. That's when I came to you with the request for a court order to dig up his remains. Then I learned that the lab keeps a DNA sample of all murder victims so I let you know the court order wouldn't be necessary.

"Our lab compared the DNA with our victim and bingo, we had a match. Although we had a name to go with our suspect, now we had to figure out how a supposedly dead man could leave his DNA on the bodies of three victims.

"We then got the results from the nail scrapings of Lassiter and they matched Robert Hale. I had detected the aroma of a woman's perfume in Lassiter's bathroom, so I figured the only logical explanation was that Hale had a female accomplice or he was a transvestite, a twin or both and that didn't sound very logical. We still couldn't connect April Langley.

"It was after Jones and I remembered how taken Lassiter was with a hospital Resident named Doctor Joanne Bentley who also worked in the Coroner's Office that it started to come together. I conferred with the Coroner, Doctor Zeller, and although he couldn't specifically remember the Hale autopsy, he did confirm that when Doctor Bentley was on duty, she would routinely assist with the autopsy and close the victim and clean up the body, usually without his presence.

"When I asked him how easy it would be for that person to extract sperm and excise skin cells undetected, he said it would only take a scalpel, a syringe and a first year medical student's knowledge of anatomy. A search of Doctor Bentley's home in Piedmont turned up a humidifier containing a vial of what we believe to be sperm and a tin of what appears to be skin cells. The DNA samples are now being tested and compared at the lab, but I'd bet my left tit they'll come back as a match."

"How the hell did…" Jonah started to ask.

"Please, let me finish," Dinosa interrupted, "Our background investigation on Joanne Bentley reveals she was adopted by her Aunt Josephine and her husband Albert Bentley after her parents were killed in a plane crash and became the sister of two younger siblings who had previously been adopted by the

Bentleys. The two younger children were adopted from the 'Sisters of Mercy' orphanage and the girl's name at the time of adoption was April Langley who later changed her name to Irene Angelia.

"Here's the kicker. Several years ago the entire family was killed in an automobile accident except for Joanne Bentley. We believe Joanne Bentley was the actual sister killed in the accident and Irene Angelia survived and assumed her sister's identity. We think this was another attempt to bury her real identity and cover-up her past crimes and any future crimes she might commit. After obtaining her adoption papers we traced her real father back to a Brian Langley who's serving a life sentence at San Quentin. A DNA test confirmed that he is the father of Joanne Bentley, aka Irene Angelia Bentley, aka April Langley.

"We requested our counterparts in Burlingame re-interview their victim's college professor slash friend and they have confirmed that he had a serious relationship with Joanne Bentley who abruptly dumped him shortly before the death of their victim. They also informed us that they didn't think they would have a problem conceding prosecutorial jurisdiction for their case to us."

Dinosa took another deep breath and continued, "So, at this time, we believe we can make a strong case and we can prosecute Irene Angelia Bentley for the murders of Susan Darden, Madelyn Davies, Sister Shari and Arnold Lassiter.

"Sister Shari, we believe, was an unwitting and innocent accomplice. She must have known and was probably the only person who knew Doctor Bentley's true identity. I mean, she knew April from the time the orphanage became her guardian when she was six years old. Knowing her troubled past, I think April's manipulating personality coupled with Sister Shari's sympathetic and nurturing nature, the good Sister kept the secret identity changes.

"We believe Doctor Bentley also murdered her adoptive parents and siblings, but making that case will be difficult. We also believe her mother, Ruth Langley was her first victim, but proving that would be almost impossible."

"Well Dinosa," Jonah Stein said gathering up the file contents, "I'd like to congratulate you and your team for conducting a fine investigation. This appears to be a cut and dry capital case. I mean, the bitch obviously planned and premeditated these crimes, she laid in wait and committed gross bodily torture and harm and for good measure she committed kidnapping during the commission of these crimes all of which will be extenuating circumstances. It'll take a little time digesting all of this information and I'll be calling you with questions from time to time.

"Actually, you conducted too good of an investigation. All of this will have to be turned over to her defense counsel and they'll use her deprived history as mitigating circumstances, but that will be a challenge I can overcome."

Stein got up and when he reached the door he looked at Kane and said, "Why are you wasting my time with such an easy case? Any number of junior prosecutors could get a conviction on this one."

After he had departed, Kane said, "God, I dislike that arrogant asshole."

Dinosa filled her water glass, walked to the window and staring out at nothing said, "Val, I know this woman just murdered an innocent dear friend and neighbor of mine and a fellow officer, not to mention her other victims. I realize she has a twisted and degenerate mind and there's no justifying her actions, but I can't stop thinking about the mitigating circumstances our asshole just referred to.

"I mean, I realize this woman is a sick vile individual and should never be released in society again. Hell, maybe the death sentence would be a humanitarian way out for her."

"What would you have me do?" Kane asked respectfully.

"Hell, I don't know. Maybe you could just keep a close eye on the prosecution and maybe, if you think it warrants it, you could intervene at an appropriate time and meet with her defense and agree on a sentence that would preclude a trial. Look at the interview video from this morning and tell me you don't think this is a very tortured lady," Dinosa said with pleading eyes.

"I'll do that, I promise," Kane replied.

* * *

CHAPTER THIRTEEN

"During your investigation of Ms. Bentley, Investigator Dinosa, did you delve into the history of my client?" the young and handsome defense attorney asked during cross examination.

"Yes," she replied simply.

"During that investigation, did you discover that the defendant was taken by the State from her mother, awarded to the Sisters' of Mercy School for Girls and subsequently adopted by Mr. Garrett Bentley and his wife Doctor Wanda Bentley?"

"Yes."

"When six year old Ms. Bentley arrived at Family Services, what condition, if you know, did they find my client to be in?"

"According to the criminal investigation report submitted jointly by CSI and the SFPD, she was dressed in dirty clothes, she was malnourished and had been recently raped," Dinosa replied.

"And do you know where her mother, Ruth Langley was found?"

"According to the same report, she was found six hours later in her bed at her residence," Dinosa said stoically.

"According to that same report, was she in bed alone and if not can you identify who it was she was with?"

"She was with a gentleman, and I'd have to refer to my notes or the report to give you his name."

"At that time, was Ruth Langley able to identify that man by name?"

"According to the report, no she could not."

"Was she arrested at that time and what were the charges?"

"Again, referring to the report, she was arrested for felony conspiracy and aiding and abetting a rape and felony neglect and abuse of a child."

"During your investigation, did you do a criminal background check of Ruth Langley and if so what did you find?"

"Objection, your honor, that's a compound question," Assistant DA Jonah Stein said standing up.

"Let's not be so trite, over ruled," the Judge remarked.

"Yes we did and found that Ms. Langley had during the previous four years, three arrests for possession of narcotics and two for prostitution," Dinosa answered.

"I'm going to replay the video of your interview with Ms. Bentley, already in evidence, and I'll have only one question for you," the Defense Attorney said.

He fumbled with the DVD player and the image of the police interrogation room appeared on the big screen. He fast forwarded it and then froze the frame just after Dinosa said, "Ah shit, Marcus will you get somebody up here from Forensic Psychology," and showed Dinosa wiping her eyes with the cuff of her blouse.

"Inspector Dinosa, are those tears you're wiping?"

Jonah Steen stood up immediately and roared, "Objection, relevance your Honor!"

"Sustained," the Judge replied.

"One last question, Investigator Dinosa, to your knowledge has my client ever described the events surrounding her rape or identify her rapist?"

"Not to my knowledge."

As Dinosa stepped down from the stand she glanced over at Irene Bentley and noticed her hair had been cut short and she sat with her head down and her hands folded in her lap. She was rocking slowly back and forth in her chair seemingly oblivious to her surroundings.

Walking toward the exit, Dinosa heard the Judge say, "At this time I'm going to dismiss the Jury for the day and ask them to follow my previous instructions and ask both Counsels to meet me in my chambers."

In the corridor outside the courtroom Valerie Kane approached Dinosa and placing her hand on Dinosa's arm, said, "It seems I've been summoned to the Judge's chambers. He's going to encourage the Prosecutor's Office and the Defense Team to work out a plea agreement."

"What the hell does that mean?" Dinosa said looking puzzled.

"It means Jonah got his day in court and you got your wish," Kane said with a wink, then added, "And it means t-a-c-t works."

The End

EPILOGUE

Chalmers and his wife Colleen found Ian and Mary sitting at the table past the bar and in the far corner at 'Lefty's Tavern'. They greeted one another and sat down. Chalmers ordered a glass of white wine for his wife and a Pilsner Ale for himself.

When their drink order arrived, Chalmers lifted his bottle and said, "Here's to Mary and her Sherlockian solving skills."

Dinosa nearly spilled her drink and blurted out with a laugh, "Sherlockian? Is that even a word?"

"And here's to life getting back to the normal, abnormal around the Dinosa/O'Farrell household," Ian added.

"Speaking of your household, and I know it's none of my business, have you guys set a date?" Colleen asked.

"Yes we have and sending out the invitations is next on our agenda. Our house will be ready to move into next month and we've set the date to get married on June sixth," Ian answered.

"Oh, that's wonderful. Where is the ceremony going to be?" Colleen inquired.

"Well, my parents want it to be a big affair in the Church and a giant reception at one of the ritzier hotels in the City, but we've decided to make it a small wedding at our beach front home with just family and our closest friends," Mary said.

"That sounds delightful and so romantic," Colleen beamed and nudging her husband she added, "We got married at one of those rental chapels in Reno."

"Great," Ian perked up, "You can be the one to tell her parents."

Dinosa's cell phone rang and turning away from the table and looking at the caller I.D., she said, "Sorry it's the boss, I have to take this."

"Hey Val, what's up?"

She stood up and walked toward a vacant area next to the hall leading to the restrooms. Colleen leaned across the table and hugging Ian said, "I'm so excited for you two, congratulations."

Returning to the table, Dinosa picked up her handbag and said, "I'm so sorry you guys. It seems some bodies are washing up on the shore at Aquatic Park and I have to go."

Looking apologetically at Ian and then at Chalmers she asked, "Chuck, could you and Colleen give Ian a lift home?"

After she left, Ian sighed, "I guess our lives are returning to the abnormal, normal."

* * *

CPSIA information can be obtained
at www.ICGtesting.com
Printed in the USA
FFOW01n0356190514
5468FF